SIN CITY SUBMISSION

SIN CITY SUBMISSION

A Doms of Genesis Novella

Jenna Jacob

Sin City Submission
A Doms of Genesis Novella
Jenna Jacob

Published by Jenna Jacob

Copyright © 2016 Dream Words, LLC
Print Edition
Edited by: Blue Otter Editing, LLC
ISBN 978-0-9864306-7-1

DEDICATION

To my amazing husband, Sean.
The unconditional love and encouragement you give
through good times and bad fill me with the strength and determination
to keep reaching for those elusive stars.
I love you.

To Shelley, for your guidance, friendship,
and most of all…your love.
Thank you.

And to you…the loyal readers who bless me with your
passionate support,
laughter, and astonishing friendship. You all amaze me.
Thank you—each and every one—from the bottom of my
heart.

Jenna

CHAPTER ONE

AVA GIBBS CLIMBED out of the quiet taxi only to be met by an onslaught of commotion. Time was money, a fact driven home by the flurry of valets and cab drivers, shuttling luggage as if they were buckets of water meant to put out a fire. Ava knew all about fires. She hadn't been able to snuff out the blaze that had been roaring inside her for over a week. A smoldering hunger her boss, Quinn MacKinnon, CEO and President of Fusion Productions—the industry leader in concert promotions—had ignited when he'd invited, or rather instructed, her to join him for a night of *fun* in Las Vegas.

Ava was neither stupid nor naïve. Dating your boss was a cliché at best and oftentimes destined to end in disaster. But Quinn was more than her boss and lover—he was her Master. A fact they kept a closely guarded secret. Even the fellow members of Club Genesis—the private BDSM dungeon where they'd met—didn't know they were living together much less fulfilling their kinky desires behind closed doors.

She sometimes missed her friends and the club, but it was a small price to pay. The sheer joy and contentment she found with Quinn couldn't compare. Even after being together for three years, the mere sight of him still made her tingle inside, and she was beyond ready to lay eyes on him again, not to mention have him fuck her senseless.

The cabbie cleared his throat, drawing Ava from her wistful musing. She tipped the driver, then tugged her suitcase behind her and into the hotel. Entering the lobby of The Nyte—Las Vegas' newest and most exclusive luxury resort—a knowing smile kicked up the corners of her lips. While she'd expected a classy and extravagant hotel, finding herself surrounded in a sphere of cascading crystal and shimmering gold took her breath away. Quinn didn't skimp when it came to indulgence; the six-foot-four, sexy Scot, with his thick spice-colored hair and intoxicating sage-green eyes, enjoyed pampering her. Ava didn't complain a bit.

Gliding deeper into the lobby, she felt her excitement blossom even more. In a matter of minutes, she'd be enveloped in Quinn's strong arms again. A part of her felt like a ridiculous schoolgirl. He'd only been gone from their sprawling estate north of Chicago for five days. Quinn had come to Vegas to supervise the kickoff tour of Splatter—a group of talented young musicians who regularly brought the rock world to its knees. But only a few short hours after he'd left, Ava had felt her focus slip away. The centered, submissive type of focus her Master instinctively bred inside her.

Weaving her way through the people in the lobby, she followed Quinn's instructions and stepped up to the front desk marked VIP. A dark-blonde-haired man with boyish lips and pewter-gray eyes welcomed her. Darting a glance at his nametag, she flashed a courteous smile at Wesley Tate, Supervisor.

"How can we help you today, pretty lady?" Wesley asked. His tone teemed with gay pride.

"I'm joining one of your guests…Quinn MacKinnon. He

asked that I see you first to give you my thumbprint." *Asked my ass. Instructed was more like it,* she thought with an inward scoff.

Wesley straightened, tilted his head to the side, and dissected her with a delving stare. "Don't tell me. Let me guess," he said, tapping a finger to his pursed pink lips.

"Guess about what?" she asked, feeling utterly confused.

"Which recording artist you are, of course."

"Oh, I'm not...I..." *For crying out loud, don't tell him you work for Quinn. He'll think you're a sleazy gold digger.* "Oh, I'm not a musician. I'm just a good friend of Mr. MacKinnon's."

"Of course you are, sugar. Why else would you be spending the night with him in our most popular suite? You lucky little thing, you," Wesley whispered with a conspiratory wink before a knowing grin speared his lips. He quickly guided her thumb to the center of the scanner before nodding toward the lobby. "The elevator is to your right. Carlos will take up your luggage."

"That's okay, I only have one—"

"Ah-ahh. No. No. No. We'll have none of that," Wesley interrupted with a chastising wiggle of his finger. "No guest of Mr. MacKinnon will carry her own luggage. I pride myself on ensuring special guests and their visitors receive five-star service, and if you need anything at all, ring the front desk and ask to speak to me directly."

"Thank you, Wesley. I'll be sure to do that."

The supervisor's eagerness was endearing. Ava flashed him a quick smile before she turned and followed the young Latino bellman to the elevator.

Carlos stood at attention in his crisp, tailored uniform as

they rode in silence. She settled her gaze on his hands, firmly clasped behind his back and concealed beneath a pair of pristine white gloves. She found it ironic. Both she and Carlos provided a service.

Though they were on opposite ends of the spectrum and some might construe their roles as menial or debased, Ava found comfort and satisfaction pampering Quinn and kneeling at his feet.

Serving her Master completed her, and being adored and loved by him was icing on the cake of her happy life. She didn't give a fig about those who couldn't grasp the concept of a power exchange.

As the elevator passed floor after floor, a flutter of anxiety bubbled in Ava's belly, pelting holes in her self-assurance. During her last conversation with Quinn, he'd made it clear that he intended to push her submissive limits at this Vegas rendezvous. Sucking in a deep breath, she glanced again at Carlos praying that when facing Quinn's tasks, she could muster the same resolve that the bellman displayed.

When the elevator stopped, butterflies swooped and dipped as the polished metal doors slid open. Placing her thumb on the keypad, Ava squared her shoulders, searched for the peaceful submissive within, and entered the suite.

Her eyes grew wide as she took in the splendor around her. The luxurious surroundings looked more like an extravagant apartment than a hotel room. The décor of soothing creams and rich earth tones did little to calm the nervous energy pinging inside her. As she stepped across the speckled marble entry, the rainbow-colored prisms from the crystal chandelier above her head danced over her feet. Were the sinfully lavish surroundings meant as a message? Did Quinn expect a comparably stunning display of her submission? Ava's anxiety soared off the charts. She needed to see him...touch him, feel his formidable calming, reassuring Dominance in a tangible way.

Breezing past the sitting area and the inviting designer furnishings, Ava sucked in a ragged breath. "Quinn?" she called, cringing at the sound of desperation in her voice.

But he didn't respond.

Semi-cognizant of Carlos following behind her Ava stopped and turned. While sliding a tip into the palm of his glove, she thanked him, then gripped the handle of her suitcase as she watched him exit the suite.

"Quinn? Are you here?" she called once more, but again, there was no reply.

A hint of his amber-musk cologne tickled her nose, and Ava followed the scent to a set of ornate pocket doors. Pulling them open, she discovered another exquisitely decorated room. A massive four-poster bed snagged her attention along with a rose, blindfold, and note that lay atop the mattress. Staring at the paper, she instantly recognized Quinn's familiar bold pen strokes.

Skimming a cursory glance over the thick oak balusters sunk into the carpet, a tiny wave of disappointment flittered through her. She'd expected to find some type of bondage apparatus attached to the bedposts. Ava loved when Quinn tied her up. Being at his mercy, bound beneath his soft, silk rope, was always a treat. He was a master of Shibari—Japanese rope bondage. Every time the pressed the shock of knots between her folds, Ava soared off into subspace. And Quinn would always send her higher by tugging on the rope that bisected her butt cheeks…teasing and toying with her mounting orgasm. Of course, his whiskey-soft, raspy voice wafting over her flesh, forbidding her to come only fueled her sexual depravation even more. A needy, hungry chill undulated up and down her spine.

Biting back a moan, Ava eased onto the edge of the mattress and drew the rose to her nose. Inhaling its sweet fragrance, she picked up the note and began to read.

My sweet princess,

Remove your clothes, lie back on the bed, and bring yourself to the brink of orgasm.

I know you'll want to come, but you don't have permission—that treat belongs to me.

When you are done, go to the bathroom and prepare yourself.

While in the tub, bring yourself to the edge once more, thinking of me licking and sucking your sweet, wet cunt.

Do not come.

Return to the bed ready to serve me…naked, blindfolded, and on your back with your legs spread wide. Play with your pretty swollen clit one last time, but remember…you do not have permission to come.

I expect to find you writhing, begging, and out of your mind with need, but you will wait for me, princess. Wait in that blissful suspended state until you hear my voice.

I have incredible pleasures in store for you.

Go. Ready yourself for me, my succulent slut. I'll be here soon.

All my love, Q.

Ava's hands trembled in anticipation as she placed the note on the bedside table. Tracing her fingertips over the soft, satin blindfold, she couldn't wait to get started. Bolting off the bed she quickly unpacked her suitcase. She had no idea when Quinn would arrive, but she wasn't going to dawdle and disappoint him. Earning his rewards was far more fun than netting his punishments.

After stripping off her clothes, she positioned herself in the center of the bed. As she skimmed her palms over her warm, yielding flesh, goose bumps peppered her limbs. Settling her hands on her breasts, Ava toyed with her nipples. She plucked and pinched the tightly drawn flesh between her fingers and thumbs as a blissful sigh fluttered over her lips. As she tugged at her heavy orbs, ribbons of pleasure tingled up her spine and spooled beneath her clit in an urgent call.

"Mercy, Quinn," she groaned. "You're asking the impossible. How am I supposed to keep from going over?"

Ava knew it would take every ounce of self-control to keep from plunging headlong into the sweet abyss. Quinn knew that, too hence his reminders not to come.

Lowering her fingers to their assigned destination, the moist heat of her pussy surged over her hand. And when her cold index finger met her sweltering folds, Ava's stomach muscles tightened and rippled as she sucked in a gasp. Rubbing tiny circles over her clit, she closed her eyes. Picturing Quinn in her mind, she imagined it was his fingers, tongue, and lips tormenting her throbbing flesh. Strumming fervently over her sensitive nub, Ava dipped two fingers into her clutching center. She arched, moaned, and whimpered as she writhed in a lurid dance beneath her own scuffing fingers.

Reaching the peak fast and hard, she hovered over the precipice. Poised like a ballerina straining on points, Ava craved to pirouette into the inveigling bliss. Thankfully the thought of defying Quinn sent a wave of panic cresting through her. With a groan of frustration, she dropped her hands and gripped the soft cotton bedspread in her fists. Beads of sweat dotted her brows. Her chest heaved as she fought to catch her breath and uncoil from the brink of disaster.

Ava didn't fare much better in the bathtub. As her need to orgasm grew, so did her irritation. Denying the roiling demand pelting her was far easier with Quinn beside her. She had little trouble holding back while gazing at his sexy green eyes, the slash of his rugged brow, and his raspy tone warning her not to come. But alone in the tub without his Dominant presence, Ava struggled to hold back her release while a bleak and hollow emptiness engulfed her.

She *needed* Quinn there to help guide her through this daunting battle of self-control. But she was on her own, which stirred a subtle hint of resentment to worm its way inside her. Why was she finding this task so damn daunting? Then, like a bolt of lightning, it dawned on her. Quinn's conniving Dominance and her overzealous libido were to blame.

"That little sneak," she groused out loud. "He hasn't let me come in over three weeks. Quinn, you devious, wicked man."

And why was Ava just realizing she'd gone so long without orgasm? "Because Quinn is a damn good Master, that's why," she chuckled.

He'd also kept her content and in her submissive frame of mind by bestowing heartwarming praise as she sated his desires. At the time, she didn't feel the need for her own pleasure when she was tending to Quinn's.

With a newfound awareness, she drained the water and stepped out of the tub. Grabbing a thick, fluffy towel, Ava dragged the plush fabric over her flesh, cringing when it chaffed her hyper-sensitized nerve endings. Patting the moisture from her mound, she feared she might detonate like a Cape Canaveral rocket if the material touched her clit. When she finished drying off, Ava strode back into the bedroom.

Gathering her courage, she yanked the comforter back and flopped onto the mattress. Tugging the blindfold in place before easing onto the cool sheets, she let her slender legs dangle off the side of the bed. The last thing she wanted to do was touch herself again. She wasn't convinced she possessed enough self-discipline to keep from soaring over the edge this time.

Her hand hovered over her mound.

He's your Master and you are his slave. You can do this. Besides, he'd rather you tried and failed than outright gave up, the voice inside her beseeched.

Determined not to fail him or herself, Ava spread her legs wide before inching a trembling finger to her cunt. Parting her pouty flesh, she began slowly circling her stiff, pulsating clit. With her brain already saturated in endorphins and dopamine, Ava didn't slide languidly toward the heavens—she catapulted like a shooting star.

In a matter of seconds, she was panting and writhing and straining to hear the snick of the door—past desperate for Quinn to arrive and save her...grant permission to satiate the demand clawing within. Holding on by sheer will alone, the only sounds Ava heard were her own panting and pathetic moans.

"Oh, god…oh, god," she chanted breathlessly, thrashing her head from side to side. "Please, Quinn. Where the hell are you? I…I can't hold on."

Without warning, a gentle breeze wafted over the slick, hot juice flowing from her center. It was almost as if someone had displaced the air around her.

Quinn. Thank heavens.

Still strumming her clit, Ava managed to stop thrashing. She held her breath, waiting for him to give her permission. But when no words were spoken, she wondered if her mind was playing tricks on her. No, even with the scorching demand rising inside, Ava's intuition told her that she wasn't alone. The air felt heavy, as if weighed with a human aura. But if it were Quinn, he would have touched her or said something to make his presence known.

Fear, icy and cold, blasted through her. The air stilled in her lungs, and she fought the knee-jerk reaction to rip the blindfold free. No, she couldn't allow her will to undermine her submission.

"Master?" she asked in a whisper laced with fear.

Her question was met with silence. Ava's heart hammered against her ribs. She inhaled a deep breath, searching for a hint of Quinn's expensive cologne, but only the scent of her heavy arousal lay pungent and tart in the air. Convinced she was being watched, her mind swam with unnerving images. Had some homicidal maniac bypassed the thumbprint security? Was some deviant gazing at her splayed out and pleasuring herself, or had Carlos returned for some unknown reason, too embarrassed to say anything? Had Quinn ordered room service to be delivered before he arrived?

The thought of some stranger observing her provocative show terrified her, but the image of a man stroking his own cock watching as she masturbated sent a rush of slickness to spill into her palm. Ava swallowed tightly. God, what was wrong with her? A wave of disgust crested through her, and she unconsciously reached for the blindfold. As her fingers met the satin fabric, an inner war between woman and submissive raged.

"Master?" she asked once more, terror rising in her voice.

Silence.

The blistering need within her had now been replaced by cold, unmitigated fear. Still, Ava was unwilling to fail Quinn or succumb to the terror clawing within. Sucking in a choppy breath, she raised her chin.

"Who's there?" she demanded defiantly. "Answer me. If that's you, Quinn...say something. Anything...please." Her brave façade crumbled and her voice cracked.

Through the deafening sound of her heart hammering in her ears, Ava heard a soft rustling of movement. Straining, she listened intently, but the barely perceptible flutter didn't repeat. Still, the pervasive feeling of another human in the room weighed even heavier in the air and Ava's fears careened into orbit.

CHAPTER TWO

QUINN STOOD AT the edge of the bed, drinking in the sight of his gorgeous submissive. Ava owned his heart, mind, body, and soul. Watching her struggle so sweetly filled him with unmitigated pride. His chest rose and a lump of emotion lodged in his throat. A part of him wanted to speak...take away the panic and chaos rolling off her in wave after potent wave. But another part of him didn't want to break the spell. Her determination to please him was an arousing, heady, and erotic sight. A sight that fed his Dominance, like a twelve-course meal.

With his gaze locked on her swollen pink pussy, Quinn unconsciously licked his lips as he watched the glistening, spicy nectar sliding down her busy fingers. She was beyond stunning. Even his throbbing erection agreed as it leapt against the zipper of his trousers, anxious to nudge between her slick, succulent folds. To press past the inviting bow of her lips and drive deep into her soft, slippery throat.

Christ, she was gorgeous, in both body and soul.

A smile tugged his lips when she defiantly called him out, but quickly faded as her voice cracked. Ava had begun to crumble...succumbing to her own fears at Quinn's drawn-out silence.

"Please...whoever is in this room with me...say something," she begged in a desperate whimper.

Ava was strong and he savored her tenacity and courage. It was only part of what made her submission such a raw and unique gift. And he drank in every drop she willingly gave, like a fine aged whiskey.

As he bent in close to her glistening pussy, her intoxicating fragrance filled his senses. Quinn's mouth watered and he grew light-headed. Every cell in his body longed to latch his lips over her freshly waxed mound and lap up every drop of her hot, spicy nectar. Tongue-fuck her into oblivion before driving balls deep inside her wicked cunt until they were both sated and unconscious. Instead, he gritted his teeth and blew out a feather-soft breath over her wet sex.

"Oh, god," she cried in a moan of defeat. "I'm scared."

Quinn's heart sputtered as he watched Ava curl into a fetal position, then burrow her face beneath her arms…hiding from the embarrassment and fears that consumed her. The sound of her sobs filled him with a potent sense of Dominance. Her tears were the ultimate treasure. A gift he coveted more than when she knelt at his feet. When Ava stripped away the exterior shell and opened her submissive soul in such a way, it filled him with hope that all aspects of the lifestyle could be attained with his alluring slave.

Quinn knew it was time to rescue his love.

Bending, he gripped the back of her neck and hauled her upright before latching a fist into her soft, brown hair. Ava cried out, struggling and fighting as he firmly guided her face to his crotch. Forcing her to inhale his scent, Quinn pressed her nose tight against his trousers and his straining cock. After drawing in the first breath, Ava instantly relaxed and wrapped her arms around his hips, fisting his pants in a death grip of salvation.

"Oh, Quinn," she murmured. "Thank god it's you. I was so scared." Her warm breath leached through the material of his pants and he bit back a growl.

"Who?" he thundered. With a fist full of her silky hair, he forced her chin to tilt upward. He smiled at the perfectly shaped O of her lips and the blindfold blocking him from her view.

"Master," Ava whispered. "I thought you were—"

"Do you have permission to speak?" Quinn barked.

Taking a step back, he regretted cutting off her lifeline, but he'd given her a taste of contentment and couldn't gamble giving her more. Drawing his free hand back, he landed two stinging blows upon the insides of her buttery-soft thighs. Quinn clenched his jaw as Ava jolted and sucked in a startled breath. Even the miniscule touch of her flesh played havoc with his control. He'd only just started putting her through her paces, and already he ached to throw all his plans aside and sate his own thrumming desires. But he couldn't. Too much was at stake. If he didn't cement their Master/sub relationship here and now, Quinn feared she might slip through his fingers. He loved her too much to allow that to ever happen.

He'd started planning this with Ava over three months ago, after realizing she'd come to expect a predictable play routine. Their sessions had grown stagnant. Something had to be done in order for them to press forward and explore a deeper level of the power exchange.

Quinn had no one to blame but himself. He'd allowed work to consume his every waking thought. He'd lost focus from where it belonged—on Ava and pushing her submissive limits.

He aimed to give her both guidance and control…something they both craved. She'd expect the usual, and for that reason alone, Quinn had to stray far from the norm. If he didn't, she'd readily hand over her power. Though that's exactly what they both wanted and needed, Quinn wanted to forge a deeper, more meaningful relationship with Ava.

In order to do that, he'd have to keep her on her toes and throw her off-kilter. She'd likely fight him most every step of the way. But the reward for them both when she finally ceded her control would make it even more delicious, for him and for her.

Her body heat surrounded him in an enticing blanket. He had to put some distance between them before he fucked up and lost his head and tossed his plans to the wind. He took another step back.

"You disobeyed me." His tone was flat and cold. She winced. "My directions were clear, were they not?"

"Yes, but I—"

"You were afraid. I know." He cut her off and watched her lips begin to tremble. "But your fears were unfounded, weren't they?"

"Yes, Master," she whispered guiltily. "I didn't mean to fail you. I simply wasn't sure who was in the room with me. My mind wandered to scary places it shouldn't have."

Quinn inched forward and fisted her silky hair. Ava straightened and sat as still as a statue as he drew a thumb over her tempting bottom lip. "Do you think I'd let anyone have free reign over you in any way?"

"No, Sir," Ava answered quickly.

"Oh, you don't, huh?" he taunted. "What if that's what I wanted? Hmm?" Quinn felt a barely perceptible tremor skitter through her body. She opened her mouth to reply, but no words came out. "What if I wanted to sit and watch while another man...or woman used you? Would you allow that? Allow some stranger to take their pleasure with you?"

"I—I don't...is that what *you* want?" she gasped. Her body tensed as if on high alert.

"Answer me."

She swallowed audibly. "We'd have to discuss...negotiate a situation like that, Sir."

"Yes, we would," he replied. "Tell me, princess...the minute you realized you weren't alone any longer, why the sudden gush from your pussy?"

A quivering breath fluttered past her lips. Her body grew more rigid as a pink hue rolled from her chest and settled on her cheeks. "I—I don't know," she answered, slightly dropping her chin.

Quinn knew she was lying. He didn't like the fact that she wanted to keep anything from him, especially her fantasies. "I think you do. I think we both do. Remember all the times I've pressed you up against the glass in my office and fucked you from behind? All those times I whisper in your ear...*I wonder who's watching us, princess. I wonder who's getting hard and wet watching me fuck your sweet, dripping pussy.* You come like a goddamn freight train, my love. You like the idea of some stranger watching you at your most vulnerable and uninhibited state. It turns you the hell on, doesn't it, princess?"

Her blush turned a deep crimson but she still remained

silent. Quinn clenched his jaw and cinched her mane even tighter. "I asked you a question, Ava."

"Yes," she replied in a murmur so low he almost didn't hear her.

Quinn bent and pressed a feather-soft kiss to her lips in reward for her sharing what he knew was an embarrassing secret...at least to Ava. For him, it was a clearing of the path he intended to forge with her, later.

With a flick of his wrist, he released her hair. "Present your ass to me, girl. Hands and knees. On the bed. Now," he snarled.

As Ava scrambled into position, he watched her tremble while she lowered her cheek to the sheet. With her smooth, milky-white orbs raised to cock level, Quinn wanted to howl. She would surely be the death of him if he didn't get inside her soon.

"I'm sorry, Master," Ava whispered.

"For what?"

"I—I don't know," she mumbled.

"Allow me to help you then, princess," he scolded with a grin, grateful she couldn't see his delighted expression. "Are you sorry for failing to follow my instructions? Or perhaps you're wanting to apologize for trying to weasel out of answering my last question. Or is it for something altogether different, Ava?"

Her shoulders sagged. Quinn was indeed keeping her off-kilter. Dangling her over the cusp of submission by calling her *princess*, yet keeping her from fully submerging into the right headspace when he called her by her given name. Again she didn't reply. He'd either disarmed her with his knowledge of her private fantasy or she was trying to devise the answer she thought he wanted to hear.

Both were unacceptable.

With a shake of his head, he drew back his hand and landed a loud, firm slap over her soft butt cheeks. Her body jolted as she let out a short yelp of surprise.

"If it's pain you want, princess, all you have to do is ask," he whispered close to her ear. "But if it's pleasure you're seeking, you're going about it the wrong way."

"No, Master. I want pleasure…I mean, I want to give *you* pleasure," she quickly amended.

He chuckled softly. Yes, he wanted that, too…eventually. "You'll please me by answering my questions without hesitation."

"I'm sorry for both," she blurted out.

"Very good," he praised, skimming his palm over the fiery red imprint left by his hand. When she purred, Quinn couldn't help but grin. "I want you to share everything with me, princess. Not just your body but your fantasies, your secrets and dreams."

He reached down, lightly tapping the insides of her thighs. Ava obliged his wordless command by inching her knees apart wider, granting him a stunning view of her swollen, wet pussy and tightly puckered rosebud. Quinn ached to ruthlessly plunder both openings, but instead he swiped a finger though her glistening folds, coating the tip with her sultry-hot slickness. Ava moaned and slowly rolled her hips as he painted the moisture over the opening of her gathered rim. Goose-bumps erupted over her flesh, and a delightful shudder quaked through her.

Moving of their own accord, his other fingers delved into her hot, slick core. He closed his eyes, savoring her heat and the quickening rising inside him. "You feel like silk, princess...soft, luscious silk," he murmured in a voice rife with hunger.

Ava whimpered. Her tunnel clutched around his slowly stroking digits. His cock was howling to be enveloped deep within her liquid walls. Grudgingly he lifted both hands away, watching with an inward growl as her passage grasped at nothing but air.

"Count for me, princess." Her entire body tensed. He wanted to chuckle. "Surely you realize you've earned a punishment."

"But I've learned my lesson, Sir," she replied with a wheedling tone.

Ah, the little minx. Wanting to forgo pain and try to coax him into giving her nothing but pleasure had Quinn wishing he'd had the forethought to hide a nice, thick paddle under the bed. But then again, he always preferred a more hands-on approach when it came to doling out Ava's punishments.

As she began counting each slap, her voice carried out loud and strong. But by the time he'd landed six and seven, her voice quivered. Quinn wanted her tears. He knew he wouldn't have to wait long. Without a proper warm-up, Ava's tolerance for pain was virtually nil. There wasn't any familiarity for her to cling to, and that's exactly where he needed her. Even before he drew his hand back for number ten, Ava was crying. Her sobs stoked that primal, visceral need to mold her even more infinitely beneath his firm and loving hands.

The sting on his palm served to sharpen his focus like a

well-honed blade. His psyche shifted into a deeper level of Dom space. Nothing existed now except Ava and the beauty of her struggling to process the pain.

Up until a few weeks ago, Quinn would have stopped the punishment and sipped her tears, and softly caressed her reddened flesh before taking her to the heavens. Of course, that's exactly what she expected him to do, but Quinn couldn't relent. This was new ground...new territory for both of them, and Ava held the key to their future. If he couldn't entice her to hand over her power, all Quinn's plans would evaporate, like smoke on the wind.

Sucking in a hopeful breath, he landed his hand over her angry red backside five more times in rapid succession. Ava lifted onto all fours, her body taut and rigid as marble. Tossing back her head, she unleashed an ear-piercing scream. Quinn issued an inward curse...he'd lost her to the pain. Every fiber in his being wanted to wrap his arm around her waist, draw her flush against his chest, and whisper praises in her ear. Instead, he placed his wide, hot palm at the small of her back, and pressed her into position once again.

Her pitiful sobs echoed in his ears, made his cock jerk, and forced him to clench his jaw. Quinn wanted to yank off her blindfold and sip the tears as they spilled down her cheeks...drink in the life force that fed his Dominance.

UNACCUSTOMED TO THIS new side of Quinn, Ava tried to analyze his harsh and uncompromising demeanor, but the blistering fire crawling down her legs and up her spine made focusing impossible. The searing pain of his spanking engulfed her and blocked out all rational thought.

She felt lost. Cast out in a furious typhoon of uncertainty on a flimsy inflatable raft. Clutching her fists in the sheet, desperate to feel his rugged body draped over her while he whispered words of praise in her ear, Ava wondered if or when she'd find solid ground once again. Any hint of reassurance would be a godsend, yet Quinn seemed determined to withhold even a sliver of security, opting instead to continue his barrage of unrelenting punishment.

Ava was consumed by the faltering feelings and an unfamiliar sense of panic swelled inside her. And for the first time ever, she contemplated using her safeword. No. Quinn was only leading her into unfamiliar territory. That wasn't enough to warrant her calling a halt to the punishment...a punishment she'd patently earned.

And if she were truly honest with herself, he wasn't giving her more than she could handle, either. The fact that he hadn't warmed her up prior to administering the punishment was what made the pain seem unbearable. In the past, he'd used paddles and, on occasion, a crop. Ava hadn't folded and sobbed the way she did now. She'd ridden the pain, encompassed by the sublime and euphoric subspace floating in her mind.

Waves of displeasure rolled off him and seemingly crackled in the air, but the choking sobs burning the back of her throat made it impossible for Ava to offer up an apology.

Suddenly, Quinn smoothed his hand over her ass. She jerked in surprise and tried to will the taut muscles to turn to liquid so she could savor his benevolence. But his light, adoring touch felt as if he were scouring the raw nerve endings of her flesh with sandpaper. Inwardly screaming in protest, Ava longed to crawl away from his touch, but that would only add to the punishment she hoped was finished. Gritting her teeth, she panted through the pain and attempted to ride the blistering waves zipping through her body.

Only when Quinn bent and began trailing tender kisses over her enflamed orbs did Ava relax. She even sighed in relief as his firm, soft lips worked their magic, assuaging the pain and turning her bones to melted butter. Yes, the worst was over; she'd paid the penance and atoned for her disobedience. And just when she thought she'd endured all the pain Quinn wished to dispense, he sank his teeth into her throbbing flesh, like a rabid dog attacking its prey. Agony exploded, rolling up her spine; her brain begged her to flee.

"Goddammit, Quinn," Ava hissed as she blindly scrambled across the bed. "What in the hell do you think you're doing?" The hateful question launched out of her mouth before she knew what she was saying.

"Excuse me, princess?" Quinn asked in a tone ripe with indignation. "Do I need to shove a big, red ball gag between those pretty lips of yours? Or maybe I should fill your mouth with my hard cock to curb any more of your recalcitrant remarks. Hmmm?"

She swallowed tightly. Though his question was rhetorical, Ava opted for his cock over the nasty, ball gag. The damn thing made her jaw ache and caused her to drool like a dog salivating over a steak. If she was to earn a sore jaw, she'd rather achieve it by worshiping his cock.

"I'm sorry, Master. I—I didn't mean to lash out like that."

"Then why did you?"

His question came from right beside her. Ava swiveled her head toward his voice, completely unaware that Quinn had moved to this side of the bed. "It's... You're doing different things to me."

"I certainly am."

The humor in his voice both perplexed and ticked her off. "I don't understand, what you're doing. What do you want from me?"

"Everything," he chuckled before his tone turned stern. "Do you trust me?"

"You know I do."

"Hmm, I'm not totally convinced that's true, sweetheart."

Quinn stroked his fingers over her cheek. Ava nuzzled into his touch. Suddenly, the questions and worries that had been pinging through her calmed and leveled out.

"It is the truth. I swear. It's just that I can't seem to find my place...my center. The feeling that I'm connected to you."

She felt his fingers slide to the edge of the blindfold before he lifted the fabric and peeled it away. Ava blinked at the harsh light as his face came into focus. His dazzling green eyes were brimmed in pride and lust but, most of all, reflected an unconditional love. All at once, her heart swelled, and the contentment she'd sought enveloped her in a blanket of peace.

"I told you I was going to push you farther than you've ever gone, didn't I?"

"Yes, Sir, but I didn't think that I'd feel so..."

"So what, my love?" he prodded.

"Lost...struggling to find my submissive place."

"But that's exactly how I want you to feel. Do you know

why?"

"No." Ava shook her head.

She sat quietly, waiting for him to explain. Explain why he aimed to shake the foundation out from under her in such an unusual and disquieting way. Tendrils of self-doubt began to web through her system. Was she lacking to provide him with the type of submission he craved? Had the failure to follow his task been as much of a disappointment to him as had been to her? Questions cluttered her mind. Ava's anxiety mounted as she patiently waited for him to say...something.

As if gathering his thoughts, Quinn pursed his lips, then flashed her a devastating smile. His eyes twinkled as he eased onto the bed beside her. Ava exhaled the boulder of tension from her lungs, and her heart sputtered. The heat of his body and masculine scent—a mixture of woodsy cologne and soap—surrounded her like a blanket of reassurance. Ava wanted to climb into his arms, curl up against his steely chest, and stay there for all time.

"A Master pushes limits, princess. It's his job. I've been neglecting my duty to you...to us. But I intend to make that up, starting here and now."

"You've not been neglecting me. You've been busy... We both have. Besides, I like the things we do. I..." Did she dare say it? "I know where I stand...what my role is, and where my place is in our BDSM relationship."

"And therein lies the problem, princess. It's time to move past the things you *like*, and push to another level to find more fulfillment than we've experienced thus far."

Ava's heart sank. In a backhanded way, Quinn confirmed her biggest fear—she wasn't meeting *his* expectations. What if she never attained the level he desired? What then? Would he kiss her good-bye and seek out another sub…one with more experience, who could make him happy?

The thought made her want to throw up.

Quinn cupped her chin, forcing her gaze. Studying her with his moss-colored eyes, he sliced her open like a scalpel. Quinn had always possessed an almost freakish ability to read her thoughts. The slash of his brow told her he'd picked up on the guilt and shortcomings that wheedled their way into her brain.

With a frown settled over his mouth, he stood and extended his hand. She stared at his wide palm and capable fingers before accepting his invitation as he helped her from the bed. His skin was hot, setting off a familiar current of electricity that tingled up her arm and sent a low vibration humming through her system.

He moved his hand to the small of her back. A ripple of delight rolled up her spine as Quinn led her across the room to a nondescript wooden door. Funny, she hadn't even noticed the portal when she'd unpacked. Of course, her mind had been focused on other things.

She watched as he lifted a small key from his pocket. With a tiny snick, the lock disengaged and the door swung open. Peering inside, Ava sucked in a gasp.

CHAPTER THREE

A HIDDEN DUNGEON unfolded before her. The scent of leather permeated her senses as she skimmed a gaze over the numerous paddles, crops, and whips suspended by individual hooks along the wall. Every type of BDSM implement, from innocuous to frightening, was at Quinn's disposal. There were several pieces of dungeon furniture, as well. A thickly padded table, spanking bench, and sturdy-looking suspension frame, but Ava's eyes stilled on the massive St. Andrews cross, situated in the middle of the room.

Her mouth went dry. While she'd experienced some of the implements in private play with Quinn, like the flogger, nipple clamps, and crop, she'd only seen some of the other toys, like whips and quirts, used on other subs at Club Genesis.

A palpable wave of Dominance rolled from Quinn's body, lending an air of formality to the atmosphere. Ava knew he'd purposefully acquired this special room for more than a relaxing session with a thuddy, heavy flogger followed by hours of lovemaking. He aimed to make their time together in the private dungeon serious and memorable.

A tiny shudder passed through her. Did she have the mettle to buck up and venture into the unknown without leaving claw marks on the drywall? She wasn't sure, but she knew she had to try to meet his Dominant needs.

"Before we begin," Quinn stated, placing his strong hands on her shoulders and turning her to face him. "I am pleased with you, princess. You bring me much joy and happiness, and the power you give me...well, I couldn't be a prouder Master."

She leveled him with a wide-eyed stare. Yes, he'd read every one of her insecurities as if she were an open book.

"This isn't a test of your submission, my love. It's simply an exploration of fantasies...yours and mine."

His words were laced in wicked promise. A flutter of confidence began to bubble inside her. "I'd love nothing more than to make all your fantasies come true, Master."

"Let's see if we can do just that then, my precious princess."

Quinn's wide, satisfied smile sent her heart racing and a sense of triumph warming in her veins. He pressed a sweet kiss to her forehead, then led her across the room to the big, polished cross. Without a word, he wrapped her wrists in fleece-lined leather cuffs. Ava's body trembled in anticipation. While he bound her ankles to the cross in another set of cuffs, she slightly mourned the loss of being bound by his soft rope. The ability to move her torso freely felt strange, and would take a bit of getting used to, but Ava sucked in a deep breath and focused on her cuffed limbs.

Peeking over her shoulder, she expected to see Quinn stripping out of his dress clothes, but instead she watched as he plucked several toys from their hooks. Stealing glances beneath her long lashes, she watched him place several items on the table beside her before he arched a brow in her direction.

"Eyes toward the front, princess. You don't need to fret over the toys I've chosen. Your job is to relax and savor the pleasure I give you." An eager smile kicked up the corners of his mouth. Moving in close, he cupped a hand to her nape, then softly massaged her tense muscles. "What is your safeword, my love?" he asked in a low, buttery voice.

"Bats." Ava had chosen that specific word based on her phobia of the nasty, winged rats.

"Very good," he praised in a loving tone. "I want you to close your eyes and relax while you open your mind. Focus on the sound of my voice and hand over your control to me, princess. I'll be with you every step of the way."

Ava issued a resolute nod, wondering when he was going to get naked. But Quinn simply remained behind her, kneading the knots from her neck and shoulders. She quickly realized he had no intention of following the patterns of the past... the systematic progression she'd grown accustomed to. She suddenly felt overexposed and uncomfortably vulnerable in a prickly way.

Relax and open your mind, he'd instructed. With an inward nod, she exhaled a calming breath. But when he stepped away, a palpable hum sang though her as she restlessly lingered...waiting for him to begin. Not knowing what he planned to do was driving her out of her mind.

QUINN TRAILED A long, slow gaze up and down Ava's naked body. She was a vision of absolute beauty. He could have stared at her luscious body cuffed to the cross for the rest of his life. But then they'd both miss out on the pleasures he planned. Still, he found he couldn't look away from the view of her stretched out…all that inviting pale flesh was a tempting canvas. She even still bore a hint of pink upon her supple ass cheeks. He found it impossible to keep from touching her again. Drawing his wide palms up and down the length of her back, Quinn began reinforcing the Dom/sub connection. Soothing and centering his girl, he branded her trust, absorbed her love, and treasured the power she relinquished all the way to his soul.

The musky scent emanating from her pussy filled his senses, making him edgy with need. Quinn continued to massage Ava's shoulders and spine, feeling her tension melt beneath his fingers until she slumped against the wooden frame.

A tiny smile tugged at his lips. He was already losing her to the lure of subspace. He was often amazed how she tumbled off so quickly, but then most everything about Ava blew his mind. No other woman understood him the way Ava did. Quinn had been around the block enough to know this gorgeous creature splayed out before him held his future in her soft, slender hands.

Leaning in, he pressed a light kiss at the base of her neck. Closing his eyes, he savored the steady pulse of her heart upon his lips. Ava exhaled a soft and blissful sigh as she seemed to further float away. It was time to bring her back to the surface, at least for a little bit, before he allowed subspace to pull her away once more.

Plucking up the paddle lined with rabbit fur, Quinn weighed it in his palm. The wide, polished wood was heavy…heavy enough to snag her attention but not vicious enough to make her climb the cross. Drawing the paddle back, he landed a quick slap to her pink cheeks. With a gasp, Ava jerked before snapping her head his direction and pinning him with a wicked glare.

He bit back a grin and gave her another swat. "Is there a problem, princess?" he asked in a taunting, lyrical tone as he petted the fur side of the paddle over her orbs.

"No. You, uh, surprised me is all," she replied nervously.

"And I thoroughly intend to keep surprising you, my love."

"So you've said," she mumbled under her breath.

"Oh, my sassy little minx," Quinn chuckled. "That attitude will cost you."

Ava groaned and turned her head back to the cross. While he loved her feisty, cheeky personality, he knew he'd been far too lenient with her in the past. Quinn didn't bother trying to hide a grin as he watched her tighten her butt cheeks in anticipation of another swat. No doubt Ava was trying to gain a foothold, but she had no idea he intended to make that an impossible feat.

With the flick of his wrist, Quinn landed the paddle against her flesh once again before assuaging the burn with the soft, silky fur. In the past, he would have slowly warmed her up before setting her free to languish in subspace. He would have untied her from the stunning Shibari knots and made passionate love until they both drifted off to sleep...sweaty and sated. But not today. Quinn planned to ride the razor's edge and push past her comfortable plateau.

Unbeknownst to Ava, the many meetings he'd attended outside the office over the past four weeks had instead been training sessions. He'd arranged for Mika LaBrache, owner of Club Genesis—the private BDSM club where Quinn had first laid eyes on Ava—to teach him how to throw a single tail. Mika had offered up his beautiful slave, Emerald, to bottom for Quinn once he'd learned to control the whip. That he'd put that much faith in Quinn's abilities made him respect the dungeon owner even more.

Quinn continued caressing her backside with the fur. Reaching over, he lifted the thick, heavy flogger to remove the single tail hidden beneath it. Gripping the cool, plaited leather, he quickly inspected the new threaded popper at the end. Rolling his wrist, he swished the long leather tongue through the air, gaining a feel of its nature. Mika had taught Quinn on several different whips, explaining that each one had its own unique and individual demeanor. Once confident with the reach and temperament of the whip, Quinn raised his shoulder and flicked his wrist, causing a deliciously wicked crack to fill the air.

"What the fuck?" Ava screeched as she jerked her head toward the sound, sending the metal couplings of her cuffs to clank and clatter against the cross.

"What did you say?" Quinn asked in a low, menacing growl. "Did I give you permission to curse me?"

"No, Sir, but...what in the he...heavens are you planning to do with that?" she sputtered.

"Why, I'm going to use it on your ass. What else would I do with it?"

"Oh, no." Ava shook her head adamantly. "I don't do whips."

"You do now," he chuckled before clearing his throat and addressing her in a formidable and authoritative tone. "Unless you use your safeword. Is that what you want to do?"

Ava took several long seconds to ponder his question then pinched her lips together and shook her head.

"Good. Now face the front. Not another word unless you need to safeword out. Understood?"

Ava shot him a curt but resigned nod. Her eyes danced with the struggle to hold on to her sense of self versus relinquishing her power. The internal tug-of-war made his blood boil with pride. Quinn ached to coax every drop of her submission.

Damn…he was crazy in love with this woman.

A visible tension had returned to her body, and her subtle shiver told him that she was scared of the whip. And that was exactly where he wanted her…unsure and taken in by her own preconceived notions of pain the toy was capable of inflicting. Of course, she didn't know any better, and it was up to him to enlighten her.

Shifting the whip to his left hand, Quinn reached back and gripped the heavy flogger from the table. With a loud thwack, he landed the wide leather tails across her ass. Ava jumped. No, that wasn't what she'd expected, and it filled him with delight. As he rhythmically slapped the soft fronds over her shoulders, back, and butt, Ava once again slumped against the cross as kitten-like purrs slid from her lips.

Guiding Ava deeper and deeper to that serene place inside her, Quinn felt himself shift into a more compelling level of Dom space once more. Everything around him began to blur and disappear, everything except Ava. He settled his focus solely on her, watching as the recoil of the flogger nudged her onto her toes. Studying every breath she inhaled and exhaled while his arm directed the leather tassels like a conductor's baton.

Once he had lured her into a false sense of security, Quinn replaced the flogger with the whip. Moving in close behind her, he snaked the cold, plaited leather between her shoulder blades. Ava sucked in a quick breath, and her body jerked as he yanked her out of her reverie. He leaned in against her back and nuzzled his face against her slender neck. Rubbing his jaw over her smooth flesh, he abraded her skin with the prickly scruff adorning his face. Her squeal of laughter echoed in his ears as she crimped her shoulders, trying to ward off his ticklish assault.

With a grin, Quinn cinched a hand in her hair, then jerked her head back. As he bathed her neck in soft kisses, biting and nipping his way up her silky flesh, Ava purred in delight. Her sweet sounds of surrender vibrated over his lips, making his eager cock jerk once again. It would be nothing short of a miracle if he didn't come in his pants like a horny teen before this session was through. Gripping the flogger once more, Quinn landed the heavy tails over and over again, leading Ava back into the blissful depths of peace.

LULLED BY THE rhythmic thud of the flogger, her anxiety over the frightening whip bled from Ava's system. She found comfort in the relaxing tempo, but every time Quinn paused, she held her breath. Poised to feel the cold, evil whip slide over her flesh again, she hoped he'd settle a sweet, enticing kiss upon her neck instead. Hands down, she preferred his kisses, but Quinn had her so off-balance she wondered if he intended to use the whip at all, or if he simply wanted to mind-fuck her to death.

You're not thinking like a sub, her inner voice scoffed.

Ava truly wanted to settle into a proper state of mind. She could, too if Quinn would simply warm her up like he usually did and take her to the heavens. Unfortunately he had other things in mind, and dammit, she wanted to know what he planned to pluck out of his bag of tricks.

Suddenly, his warm breath breezed over the side of her neck. Ava closed her eyes. Yes. Yes. This is what she wanted…Quinn's tender, loving, passionate side. She breathed in his reassuring masculine scent, and the ground beneath her grew stable, solid, and secure. Turning her head, she offered him her lips. But when he didn't kiss her, Ava lifted her heavy eyelids. He stood staring at her. His sage-colored eyes had turned dark and permeated with a clit-throbbing hunger she wanted to satisfy.

"Expecting something, princess?" he taunted as a wicked smile of delight lit up his face.

"I need a kiss, Sir."

"Hmm, is that so?"

"Please," she begged, hoping he would oblige her request.

"No." He shook his head, effectively plucking the hope from inside her. "Let go, Ava. Take what I give and stop trying to top from the bottom. You're not in control of this session: I am, and you're making my job harder than it needs to be."

"I'm not topping from the bottom," she argued with a disgruntled pout. "You always kiss me when I need it."

"Ah, but do you really need a kiss, or simply want one?" His cinnamon brows furrowed.

All right, so she wanted one. When had that become a crime? "I'm not trying to be difficult. It's just that…I'm struggling here…Sir."

"I know you are, but I've no intention of submitting to you while you try dictating my Dominance."

Though his words were spoken softly and filled with love, Quinn's message came through loud and clear.

"I know. I'm trying. I really am."

He pressed a feather-light kiss at the corner of her mouth. It technically wasn't even a kiss. But it would have to suffice since she knew better than to ask for more.

"Try harder for me, princess," Quinn whispered before placing his palm on the top of her head and directing her to face the cross once more. "Trust me, Ava."

"I do. You know I do," she murmured.

"Prove it," he challenged.

Closing her eyes, she drew in a deep breath, then exhaled slowly, repeating the process over and over. She hoped it would calm the riotous anxiety spinning through her while giving him the level of trust he desired. Ava knew in her heart she had nothing to fear, but her brain wasn't cooperating. While he'd dragged her outside the box of their usual D/s play, Quinn had long ago proven himself a capable Master. His command over her and the aftercare he bathed her in after each session completed her. His sublime affection made her heart constantly soar. Still, she struggled now to let the submissive inside hand over her staunch control.

She'd been conditioned to lead. As senior vice-president of Fusion Productions, Ava juggled a tremendous amount of responsibility. Not only did she secure multimillion-dollar contracts, but Ava had earned a reputation as a cutthroat negotiator. Only Quinn knew which buttons to push to release the pressure her VP role created. And he was the only one she'd ever let put her in such a vulnerable position. His Dominance offered her freedom. Quinn could effortlessly remove the burdens from her shoulders while providing a net of safety in the process. Ava longed for that…longed to feel both small and treasured…ached for the revitalizing and invigorating rebirth he never failed to grant her. So why was she balking at that now?

Hand it over to him, a little voice inside her pled. *Let him take it all away.*

Inwardly repeating the words of her subconscious, Ava turned them into a mantra while Quinn compelled the same motivation with the flogger. It wasn't long before the grip on her control lessened. The rhythmic falls landed harder against her flesh, lifting her higher off the floor with the force. A scrumptious burn warmed her ass as she slipped further and further into the familiar abyss of serenity. Her breathing turned shallow. Thick, feminine juice trickled from inside her and clung to her aching, swollen folds.

"That's my sweet slave," Quinn crooned in a low, coaxing whisper. "Give me your control, princess. I'll keep you safe."

Time and space seemed to slow. Even her thoughts processed like slow-churning molasses while the sounds of the flogger fell distant and muffled. The scent of her own spicy arousal hung in the air like a moist and heavy blanket of need. Suspended and floating like a rowboat lost at sea, Ava slowly realized the flogging had stopped. Forcing herself to rise up from the depths, she didn't get far before Quinn's capable fingers dipped between her legs, spreading her slickness over her pulsating clit. Ava rolled her head to the side with a mournful whimper.

"Yes. This is this what you want, isn't it, princess?" Quinn asked in a tempting whisper as he pressed a tender kiss beneath her ear.

A shiver slithered up her spine, and the heat of his body enveloped her. "Yes," she moaned, arching her back to rub against his crotch. He stood perfectly still...didn't reward her with his thick, hard cock plunging deep inside her empty tunnel.

"Such a needy little minx," he softly chided before pulling away, taking his alluring heat, captivating lips, and enticing scent.

Ava wanted to cry out in frustration, but before she could open her mouth to protest, a feather-soft kiss brushed the left cheek of her ass. Immediately another stroke whispered upon her other orb. Wading through the fog suffusing her brain, Ava realized the absence of his body heat told her Quinn's lips weren't anywhere near her. Some type of toy she'd never experienced was responsible for the wispy sensation. But she had no idea what. Surely the soft, soothing kisses weren't coming from the whip...were they?

Darting a daring glance over her shoulder, Ava's heart clutched, then began to thunder in her chest as Quinn raised the long, braided leather into the air and flicked his wrist. The whip coiled like a slithering snake before the thin threaded end whisked over her flesh with barely a sigh. The indulgent sensation clashed with the sight of the wicked whip. Ava couldn't wrap her head around the incongruent impressions warring within.

Quinn pinned her with an unhappy expression before dropping his arm. Eating up the distance between them, he gripped her chin, forcing her gaze. "Were you instructed to watch me, princess?"

"No Sir."

"Then why are you?"

"I—I wanted to see what you were using on me."

"Should it matter?"

With an inward curse, Ava shook her head. Dammit, why did she continue to challenge him? Why couldn't she simply accept what he gave and float away once more? Her own hardheadedness irritated her. She could only imagine how annoyed Quinn must feel. How long would it be before he uncuffed her and called an end to their session? Probably not much longer. The thought filled her with dread.

No. She wanted this…needed to prove to them both that she could give more than she had in the past. Needed to prove that she trusted him. Quinn's warm breath at her ear drew her focus back where it belonged.

"The whip is nothing like you expected, is it, princess?"

"No, not at all." She shook her head. "I was afraid it would rip my skin open."

"I have no desire to be a sadist, my love."

"Thank god," she replied on a grateful sigh.

"Now that you know how I intend to use the whip, do we need to discuss this further?"

"No, Sir."

"Good. Then close your eyes and let me take care of you."

As she complied, Quinn landed a sharp slap over her ass. She arched back in surprise, and he plucked her nipple, twisting it with a low growl, sending a sensual burn to spread through her. The opposing stings collided in Ava's midsection to throb in time with her aching clit. Quinn snaked his fingers between her legs and toyed with her sex once again. As he assuaged the sting, Ava felt the burn merge into a hungry quickening she wanted prolonged. Plunging two fingers inside her quivering tunnel, he rubbed her distended clit with his thumb while skimming tender kisses along her neck. As he nibbled on the lobe of her ear, Ava rocked against his hand, soaring high in a matter of seconds.

"Yes…yes," she moaned, hovering on release.

"You don't have permission," Quinn warned with evil delight.

"Please…I need…need to come," she panted breathlessly.

"Oh, you will, gorgeous. When I decide it's time. Unfortunately that time isn't now."

His denial echoed in her head as he removed his fingers. When he took a step back, irritation clawed through her. "No. No. No," she whimpered only to have her pitiful sounds of despair met with Quinn's soft chuckle.

Ava frowned. He enjoyed the fact that she was suffering…enjoyed it far too much.

Suck it up, cupcake. He can't keep you cuffed here forever.

The thought flittered through her mind, followed by a feeling of sadness that she couldn't quite put her finger on. She wanted to please him, not brood and sulk because he wasn't giving her exactly what she wanted. The cuffs might be chaining her body but not her mind. It was past time she set her inner submissive free.

When she felt the whip feathering over her backside once more, Ava's eyes slid shut. *Let go. You're safe. Treasured. Loved.* As she repeated the mantra in her head, she slid back into the peaceful darkness, lulled by the rhythmic whisper of the whip.

CHAPTER FOUR

QUINN FELT FRUSTRATED that Ava fought her surrender, though it wasn't a total surprise. Unlike him, she'd not had time to prepare for any of this. He'd purposely kept his plans a secret, wanting to both gauge and absorb her unguarded and honest reactions. He wanted to see just how far she was willing to go in order to grow.

Ava didn't like change all that much, hence her struggle now. But Quinn had an even bigger surprise in store for her, one he hoped she would ascertain at dinner. This session was but a precursor...a small stone on the road. She'd soon be scaling a mountain if all went as intended. But first he had to annihilate the barrier she slid between them before his grand plan was revealed.

Summoning all the patience he could muster, he remembered how she'd fought his Dominance in the beginning. Ava hadn't been a member of Club Genesis long when he'd first met her. She hadn't scened with any other Dominants, only gained an understanding of the lifestyle by watching others. It wasn't until he'd managed to give her a taste of subspace that she'd finally handed over her control. And her power was a heady, delightful gift.

He wanted to kick his own ass for not pushing her limits all along, but like a fool, he'd let work commitments rob him of his Dominant focus…Ava. He meant to fix that here and now.

Though she obviously hadn't yet grasped his design, Quinn held out hope that before the night was through, she'd comprehend the meaning of his strategy. He'd continue to reinforce his presence and command in order to show her how epic their journey could be together.

Quinn didn't give credence to the little voice inside his head warning this could all backfire in his face. Clenching his jaw in determination, he set the whip down and eased his chest firmly against her back. He felt a slight quiver ripple through her as he drank in the enticing heat pouring off her slender body. Quinn closed his eyes and inhaled a deep breath. The scent of her spicy, slick cunt toyed with his senses. Parting his lips, he could almost taste her on his tongue…sweet, warm, delicious. He wanted to groan in frustration but instead pressed his lips against her shoulder as he reached between her legs. Liberally coating his fingers with her fiery essence, Quinn trailed fragile, soft kisses down her shoulder blades as he inched his way to his knees.

Ava's beguiling purrs and moans spurred him on even more. Mesmerized by the sight of her red-stained orbs, he dipped lower still. Peppering kisses over her crimson flesh, he paused and parted the cheeks of her ass with his thumbs. The sight of her tiny, puckered rosebud made his cock scream. Every fiber in his being shouted for him to release his dick and drive balls deep into her sinful, puckered passage. Denying himself the wicked pleasure of squeezing his throbbing crest through her gathered opening was sheer torture.

But the poor bastard was at the mercy of Ava's submission.

A fact that had him briefly wondering who was submitting to whom.

Leaning in closer, he extended his tongue before flicking the tip over her crinkled rim. Ava issued a mournful groan that morphed into a whimper of approval as she melted against the cross. Quinn issued an inward curse of frustration. Replacing his tongue with a thumb, he craned his neck, spreading open her slippery labia with his other hand before extending his tongue and lapping at her dripping nectar.

With his thumb pressing through her tiny opening, Quinn felt the muscles in her legs tremble against his wide shoulders. And when he extended his tongue to focus on her clit before sliding two fingers into her quivering pussy, Ava cried out in ecstasy.

THE FEEL OF his tongue, lips, fingers, and heated breath engulfing Ava's sex set her ablaze. The conflagration of sensations lit her up brighter than all the lights in Vegas. Demand clamored up her spine and spread like lightning through her limbs. The decadent tingle splintered the ethereal clouds of subspace. But Ava didn't mind...didn't mind one damn bit. She tried not to focus too keenly on the overload of pleasure he capably gave, but the blistering need rising inside her was more than she could contain. She prayed Quinn would grant her permission. But the quickening buzzing inside flooded her system. The familiar numbness spread from her core and down her thighs.

"I can't... hold—"

"Come for me, princess," Quinn snarled against her pulsating pussy.

The vibration of his words over her flesh combined with his luridly thrusting fingers and invading thumb ignited her toward the heavens like a rocket. Ava screamed out his name as ecstasy had her splintering into a million convulsing shards. Her cunt clutched and milked at his fingers as her cries echoed off the dungeon walls.

Before she could begin to slide back to earth, Quinn stood and moved in close behind her. The metal teeth of his zipper sent a new wave of relief to spread through her.

"Beg for it, baby," Quinn demanded in a hoarse and needy tone.

"Please…fuck me, Master," she panted, breathlessly.

"Louder," he growled.

"Fuck me. Fuck me hard," she screamed. "I need your cock slamming deep inside me…please."

Quinn exhaled a curse. He gripped her hair roughly with one hand while he aligned the fat head of his cock against her quaking pussy with the other. With a feral, unmerciful thrust, he drove himself deep inside her. Pain fused with pleasure, and Ava cried out as she worked to accept his invading girth.

"How hard do you want it, princess?" he whispered in an animalistic tone. His warm breath cascading over her ear and down her neck sent a shiver through her. "You feel so goddamn perfect…so hot and silky. I could stay inside your tight little cunt forever."

"I don't care," she panted, needing him to move…needing to feel the friction of his shaft sliding in and out of her sweltering core. "I just want to please you, Master. Take me any way you'd like, but please...I need it now."

Though he'd pinned her whole body against the cross, Ava rocked her hips, bumping her pelvic bones against the unyielding wood. She'd probably be wearing bruises by morning, but she didn't care. The only thing she wanted...no, needed, was for Quinn to drive his delicious hard cock in and out of her and relieve the blinding pressure burning inside.

"You need it? Need what?" he taunted, nipping at the fluttering pulse point at the crook of her neck.

Ava issued a mournful groan as she rocked her ass against his steely abs.

"That's not an answer, princess. Do I need to get the whip back out?"

"No," she cried. "Oh, god. Help me, Master. I'm dying here."

"Help you with what?"

His derisive tone and maddening mind games were driving her insane. "Fuck me, goddamnit," she barked. "Move."

"Who makes the rules here, girl?" he asked, sinking his teeth into the tender flesh below her earlobe.

The frustration of the moment tried to yank her from where she wanted to be, but Ava clawed her way and held on. "You do, Master," she whimpered as a tear trickled down her cheek.

"Then tell me what you need...the right way, slave."

His whiskey-rich inveigling tone dripped over her flesh like thick, warm honey. Ava closed her eyes as a needful whimper rolled over her tongue. "Please...fuck me, slow and deep. The burn is too much. I'm going up in flames. I need you to put this fire out. *Please*. No one can make it better except you."

His satisfied hum tickled the rim of her ear as he eased, inch after agonizing inch, from inside her. Ava issued a sigh of relief only to suck in a gasp as Quinn drove himself deep once again. Mewling, she met his thrusts as a new kind of burn enveloped her. A magical, mystical heat that melted her bones and engulfed her in a fiery blaze.

Ava's head swam. Her body sang. And Quinn pumped past her quivering muscles with a tantalizing and demanding rhythm. He claimed more than her body…he claimed her soul. And she was more than happy to give him that…give him her all. Gone were her reservations, insecurities, and doubts. They'd been replaced by a glorious completeness—a euphoria that only Quinn could give.

"Yes. Oh, god…yes," she gasped, gripping the edges of the cross.

Ava held on tight as he drove her back up with each rhythmic, feral thrust. His hot breath spilled over her neck. Quinn's woodsy cologne mingled with the heady tang of sex in the air, driving her need high and hard. Even the fact that Quinn was still fully clothed and the metal of his zipper that chaffed her enflamed orbs didn't distract from the euphoria suffusing her. The symbolism of her being stripped bare didn't escape her, either, and understanding seeped into her lust-filled haze.

Quinn wasn't making love to her, at least not in his usual way. No, he had a purpose for this raw, animalistic act of sex. She simply didn't know what it could be. Ava's body began to tense. God, she didn't want to fail him…not again. Sensing the change in her, Quinn drove deep inside her, then stilled. He burrowed his face against the slope of her neck, dragging his whiskers over her flesh, before trailing his tongue up the side of throat close to her ear.

"Come back to me, princess. Get out of your head. Follow where I lead you," he murmured in a patient and loving tone.

Lifting her chest from the cross, Quinn wrapped both arms around her and pulled her tight against his rugged body. Surrounded in his decadent heat, she was disappointed by the barrier of clothing separating them. Still, Ava took refuge in his strong arms. He silently held her for several minutes before reaching up and releasing the metal carbine that bound her to the cross. Quinn then clasped each of her wrists and drew her arms down to her sides. Slowly withdrawing himself from inside her, he bent and released the cuffs at her ankles. A wave of panic crested through her. She'd done it…failed to surrender her all to him. Tears stung the backs of her eyes, and Ava desperately tried to blink them away.

"I'm sorry," she whispered, her voice cracking with re-morse.

"Shh," Quinn instructed. "You have nothing to be sorry for, princess. You've pleased me, immensely."

"But…you didn't finish, Master."

"No. Not yet, at least." Smirking, he spun her around to face him and began removing the cuffs from her wrists. "We're just taking a little break."

"A-a break?" she stuttered, utterly confused.

"Yes. If we continue playing, we're going to miss our dinner reservations," he explained, still wearing an evil grin. "Go into the bedroom. There's a present for you under the bed. I'll meet you there after I clean up the dungeon."

Quinn's words slowly sliced through the pool of raging estrogen and angry endorphins plowing through her system. *A break? Dinner? Is he fucking kidding?* Forcing a nod while trying to mask her irritation, Ava turned and marched into the bedroom. Tossing a glance over her shoulder, she watched as Quinn zipped his trousers and gathered up the toys before depositing them into a dark, cloth bag. She was unable to fully process what had just transpired, and an oily film of defeat settled deep in her bones while his words of praise rubbed her raw.

With the conflicting emotions warring, Ava knelt beside the bed and pulled out a large white box with a huge pink bow. After setting the gift on the bed, she carefully untied the ribbon and lifted the lid before peeling back several thin layers of white tissue paper. When the contents came into view, she sucked in a gasp and fell in love with Quinn all over again.

"Mercy," she whispered as she lifted the breathtaking, champagne-colored evening gown from its box.

Her heart raced with excitement. She darted a glance at Quinn still tidying up the dungeon and couldn't help but smile. How had he known she'd been coveting this exquisite creation for months? The amazing man had spent a small fortune on the gown. With a trembling finger, she traced the tip over the delicate lace embroidery, caressed the rippling beadwork. She sighed with delight at the feel of the silky satin draped and elegantly tucked upon the seductive sweetheart neckline.

Turning toward Quinn once more, she found him leaning against the doorframe across the room. His eyes sparkled, and a devastatingly handsome smile adorned his sensual mouth. A palpable current of lust rolled off his body, drawing her attention from the dress to the lingering desire still thrumming inside her. While she didn't completely understand the rules of the game Quinn was playing, Ava had a bit of reciprocal torment to share. Easing off the bed, she strolled toward him, rolling her hips with each languid step. Quinn's smile grew wider as he pushed off the doorframe, meeting her in the middle of the room.

"Thank you for the amazing dress, Master. It's gorgeous,"

Quinn cupped her face and pressed a raw, hungry kiss on her lips. "Spoiling you is a treat, my beautiful girl. I can't wait to see you in *and* out of it. I plan to peel it off your sexy body later…with my teeth."

"I can put it on right now, if you'd like?" she countered with a playful smirk.

Kissing her again with a low growl, Quinn slid his hands to her stinging butt cheeks, then lifted her, pressing his bulging erection against her. Ava purred into his mouth, then ground her mound over his luscious hardness. She knew her playfulness would cost her. And it did. He raised a hand from her ass and landed a reprimanding swat as she clenched her cheeks together. The burn spread over her flesh like hot embers in the wind. Yet, still meshed with his mouth, Ava couldn't help but giggle. That only earned her another spank, but this time she didn't laugh, she moaned.

"That's more like it," he growled with a smile before dipping his head and latching on to one of her nipples.

"Mmm," she moaned. Arching her back, she lifted her breasts in offering.

God, she loved him more than life itself. And when he took control of her—well…when she let him—nothing on earth could compare to the unadulterated bliss he so effortlessly gave.

He drew his tongue around her areola in slow, languid

circles. Ava could feel her nipples growing impossibly harder. And when he sank his teeth into the taut berry tip, she sucked in a gasp and tangled her fingers into his soft, thick hair, basking in the sweet ache spreading over her chest. He released his mouth with an audible pop. She followed his gaze and dropped a stare at her red and distended, glistening wine-colored nipple.

"Take that sexy red ass of yours to the tub while I grab a shower. We need to leave the room in forty-five minutes."

"Yes, Sir." She smiled. "Thank you again for the beautiful dress."

"Anything for you, my princess," he replied in that low, rough voice that never failed to send a shiver down her spine.

Drawing her bath, Ava sat on the edge of the huge whirl-pool tub, watching as Quinn stripped off his clothes. She wanted to weep at the beauty of his thick-corded muscles rippling from his shoulders, down his back, and all the way to his strong, thick arms. But as soon as he stepped out of his trousers, his beautiful engorged cock snagged all her attention. It was long, hard, and lined with thick, throbbing veins, and Ava wanted to crawl to his feet, rise to her knees, and suck him deep into her watering mouth.

"I know what you're thinking, my love. The answer is no," Quinn said with a chuckle. "If you behave during dinner, I might have a special treat in store for your dessert."

"Oh, trust me, Master. I'll be a perfect angel."

He chuckled harder and shook his head. "That remains to be seen," he teased.

With a playful pout, Ava flipped on the jets and stepped into the tub as Quinn turned and made his way into the shower.

CHAPTER FIVE

BENEATH THE HOT spray and the billowing steam, Quinn issued a low curse. After forcing himself to pull out of Ava's snug little cunt, he suspected his throbbing cock wouldn't forgive him for a couple of centuries. Alone behind the frosted glass of the shower, Quinn found his own private hell. He desperately wanted to wrap a tight fist around his screaming dick and relieve the pressure before his skin split wide open. With a shake of his head, he denied himself once more, opting to let Ava eventually sate the fire churning in his balls.

After stepping from the shower, he wrapped a towel around his waist before peeking into the bedroom. Ava stood in front of the mirror, skimming a slender hand over the dress and down the sensual flare of her hips. The gown clinging to the sinful curves of her body looked erotic as hell. Still unaware she was being watched, Ava tugged the matching evening gloves up past her elbows, and he smiled.

"Why on earth did he buy me gloves?" she muttered. "They're as soft as velvet, but I can't wear my rings."

Quinn cleared his throat, grinning as she started and spun toward him. "It's a test."

"A test?" Her brows furrowed.

"Yes. You'll understand…eventually, I hope," he answered

cryptically on purpose. Moving in behind her, he held her gaze in the mirror. "You look alluring...stunningly enchanting, my love."

A blush climbed up her chest and settled on her cheeks. "Thank you, Master. This dress...it makes me feel like Cinderella. It's gorgeous. I can't thank you enough."

He smiled proudly before pressing a sweet kiss on the back of her neck. Only then did he realize she'd tucked her long chestnut curls up on the back of her head. Only a few swirling tendrils spilled from the elegant arrangement. They tickled his nose as he breathed in her sweet scent.

"Seeing you in the gown is thanks enough, and trust me—you're far more gorgeous than Cinderella, princess."

Drinking in a long, zealous look at his girl, Quinn grudgingly stepped back and began to don his black tuxedo. He could feel her eyes boring into his back as he made his way into the dungeon once again. With a grin, he snagged the items he wanted, hiding them behind his back as he turned and strolled into the bedroom.

"Would you like to wear this to dinner for me, princess?" he asked, holding out a fat latex butt plug and a tube of lube.

Ava's eyes grew so wide Quinn nearly burst out laughing. Instead, he bit the inside of his lip to maintain a somber expression.

"Do I have a choice?" she choked out, eyeing the plug dubiously.

"Of course. You always have a choice, Ava. This aspect of our relationship will never work if it isn't consensual."

A pensive expression crawled across her face as she darted several glances between him and the toy. He could almost hear the thoughts stampeding through her head...see the indecision flickering in her pretty hazel eyes.

"I will wear the plug to dinner if that's what you want, Master."

"Ah, but I didn't ask what *I* wanted, girl. I asked what *you* wanted." He watched her mouth open and close as if afraid to give him the wrong answer. Quinn frowned and pinned her with a steady gaze. "And I expect you to give me the truth."

As if he'd driven a sledgehammer through a frozen lake, the tension drained from her body, and she quickly licked her lips.

"The truth is...no. I don't want the plug anywhere near me. And I especially don't want to try and enjoy a romantic dinner with you with that...thing shoved up my butt."

"Very well." Quinn nodded as he placed the lube and plug on the nightstand next to the bed. "We'll save it for after dinner then."

Ava paled but nodded as a look of anxiety skittered over her face.

"I'll help keep your mind off the plug, princess. I promise." Quinn couldn't hold back a smile any longer. He'd keep her thoughts occupied...very occupied. "Shall we go?" he asked extending his arm.

Inside the posh elevator, he noticed Ava rubbing the tips of her glove-covered fingers together. Reaching out, he threaded his hand through hers. Being unable to touch her skin felt foreign to him, and no doubt to Ava, as well. What he planned next would be equally alien for them both, but Quinn was dying to see how she would respond.

As they made their way toward the restaurant, he spread a wide hand at the small of her back. The Dominant inside him roared at the purely possessive claim, and a confident smile tugged the corners of his mouth as they stepped to the maître'd podium. Quinn watched as Ava skimmed a glance over the empty tables. Her delicate brow furrowed as she realized they were the only customers in the place.

"I reserved the entire restaurant for us tonight, princess."

"You what?" she gasped as her eyes grew wide. "Why?"

"I wanted all your attention to myself, love."

Ava nodded numbly as Dominique, a short, portly man in a well-tailored suit, greeted them. "Ah, Mr. MacKinnon. It's a pleasure to see you again. The table you requested is ready. If you'd please follow me."

"Thank you, Dominique." Quinn nodded.

As he slid his arm around Ava's waist, they followed the maître'd up three low stairs to a large, round table situated in the center of the room. All the surrounding tables had been removed per Quinn's request. He darted a quick glance at the long white tablecloth that hugged the carpet, as a sly smile played over his lips.

He helped Ava into her chair, and he leaned down close to her ear. "Make me proud, pet."

She snapped her head in his direction, gazing up at him with a quizzical expression, then banked her confusion with a courageous nod. A rush of hope filled him. Ava seemed to be coming around quite nicely. He was already proud of his girl, but her real test was about to begin.

No sooner had Dominique turned to leave than the young waiter, Brice, appeared with an icy-cold bottle of champagne. Quinn had been very specific with his instructions when he'd met with the two employees the day before. Discretion was the better part of valor, and he felt confident his unusual requests would be honored. Without a word, Brice filled their glasses and retreated.

Quinn raised his flute and flashed her a broad smile. "A toast, to the single most amazing, and beautiful woman on the planet. My sweet, succulent Ava."

A shy smile curled at the corners of her mouth as she tipped her glass to his toast and took a sip. The sweet effervescence fizzed on his tongue and tickled the back of Quinn's throat as he swallowed.

Ava then raised her glass with a mischievous smile. "To the most handsome and loving Master on the planet."

A breathless quiver fluttered over her lips before she clinked her glass to his. Quinn tossed back a healthy gulp and set the empty flute on the table. He studied her for a long minute as his Dominant desires smoldered hot and deep.

"Come stand next to me for a minute, princess," he instructed with a wicked smile.

QUINN'S LOW, DECADENT command slid over Ava's skin. She swallowed tightly as she set her glass on the table. The tips of her gloved fingers still held the chill of the crystal, and she struggled to keep from peeling the material down her arms and off her hands. Being unable to feel any texture at all was curiously maddening.

Rising to her feet, she was all too aware of Quinn's feral gaze. As she made her way around the table, she paused, unsure if she was to kneel or remain standing. Butterflies took flight in her belly as she awaited his instructions.

Without a word, Quinn slid his hand down the satin fabric of her dress. Bending, he pinched the hem between his finger and thumb. "You look simply edible, love," he whispered before fully lifting the front of her gown.

In a rush of embarrassment, Ava reached out to grab his wrist but paused and squeezed her hand into a fist. Her heart slammed against her ribs as Quinn continued bunching the front of her dress around her waist. Panic rose like a flooding river as she quickly darted a nervous glance over her shoulder.

"I have you facing me so that no one can see what I'm doing, princess," he murmured, gazing up at her. "So you can wipe that look of terror off your face."

The hint of annoyance conveyed in his tone filled Ava with regret.

"Have I done something that's caused you to take back your trust...your submission, girl? If I have, I demand to know what it is."

Ava blinked in surprise. "No, Master," she answered vehemently as she shook her head. "You've done nothing of the sort. I trust you...trust you with my life. I've not taken back my submission...not at all."

"You act as if you have."

"I'm sorry. I don't mean to disappoint you or make you think I'm unhappy. It's just that...I'm floundering here. I know I'm fighting my submission, but it's not intentional. I swear."

"What do you need me to help you with, girl?" he asked, smoothing his free hand up the insides of her thighs and making her quiver. "What's it going to take for you to hand over all that feisty power?"

Ava tried to concentrate, but Quinn's warm caress, coupled with her fear the waiter would return and find her dress bunched to her waist with her bare pussy exposed, made it impossible. He'd definitely kept his promise to push her further.

Closing her eyes, she drank in the soothing warmth of Quinn's wide, capable hands, desperately searching for a fragment of submissive peace. But her thoughts were consumed with visions of the waiter tiptoeing up beside them, watching as Quinn touched and fondled her bared flesh. A heightened sense of arousal took hold of her, successfully snuffing out all hint of the embarrassment she'd felt earlier. *What is wrong with you?* the little voice in her head scolded. *Being watched can't seriously turn you on...can it? Where's your sense of decency?*

Obviously it turned her inside out, because Ava's modesty had suddenly left the building. She whimpered as Quinn's fingers inched higher up her thigh. His knuckles wisped over her aching folds in a feather-light brush. Her whole body quivered from his torment, and she held her breath, waiting for him to plunge his fingers deep inside her wet center. Why had she vacillated back in their private little dungeon? And why did it take the thought of being watched to break her from the inner chains that bound her?

Because you're a kinky little freak who'll break Quinn's heart if he suspects you're turned on by others watching you being aroused, her conscience volunteered, uninvited.

Suddenly Quinn landed a hard slap on the mound of her pussy. Ava's eyes flashed open wide in alarm before she quickly darted another glance over her shoulder.

"I'm waiting for an answer, girl," Quinn barked, frowning as he followed her line of vision. "I told you no one could see you, princess. Do you think I'm lying?"

"No, Sir," she hastily replied. "I—I don't know what it's going to take, Master. But I don't want to fail you."

"Oh, I think we both know exactly what it's going to take, my precious slave." Quinn's eyes held a mischievous, knowing glint. "Should I call our waiter, Brice, out to join us for a bit…hmmm?"

Ava's mouth fell open and her heart clutched before pounding in triple time. Without a word, she shook her head vehemently.

"Aw, pet. Don't be embarrassed. You like being watched, which is a good thing, because I do enjoy showing your stunning submission off." Quinn slid a finger to her clit and rubbed ever so gently. "The only way you can fail me is by not trying. Now, spread your legs for me, gorgeous. I want to see my pretty pussy framed by your dress…framed by all that satin and lace."

Ava automatically spread her legs as shock recoiled through her brain. How in the hell had Quinn known that she'd been fantasizing about the waiter watching them?

"And who knows, maybe Brice will return and you can show him how breathtakingly beautiful my sweet sub can be."

A wave of excitement rushed through her veins. Quinn wasn't angry over her naughty little fantasy…he encouraged the insanity. God in heaven, what on earth was she doing? The mortifying thought rolled through her brain as she stared, slack-jawed, at Quinn.

"You can do this for me, Ava. But most of all, you can do it for yourself…for us. This is just the first step I have planned for you. Trust in me, love. I won't fail you. I won't fail us."

The passion and promise in his voice struck a place deep inside her…a part of herself she hadn't known existed until now. Filled with a sense of self-assurance, Ava felt tears sting the backs of her eyes, felt her heart expand, and felt a sense of peace warm every cell in her body. Determination bubbled to the surface. Quinn wanted her unadulterated trust, her power, her heart, mind, body, and soul. Come hell or high water, Ava was ready and willing to hand all she was and could be over to him.

Ava tossed away all doubt and suffused herself in the glory of being Quinn's slave.

Suddenly, she realized she didn't need or even want the waiter returning to witness the things Quinn was doing to her. He'd fulfill all her fantasies. Quinn would protect her, keep her safe, and treasure her in all ways.

"I give you all of me, Master," she whispered as she reached up and cupped his chiseled cheek.

"That's my girl," he murmured. The tips of his fingers continued to toy with her folds, making her tremble. And when he pressed harder against her clit, Ava cried out. She didn't care if there were one or a thousand people in the room—her focus was on Quinn, and only him. Repositioning his hand, he delved two fingers inside her clutching tunnel. Sparks ignited and burst behind her eyes as he used his thumb to tease and torment. Ava clutched the hem of her dress and closed her eyes, basking in the tingles that skittered through her.

"So hot. So soft. So fucking silky," Quinn uttered before bending to glide his warm lips up her thigh.

Ava released one hand from her dress and sank her fingers into his hair. Inwardly cursed the gloves that kept her from feeling the texture of his thick cinnamon mane.

"The scent of your cunt is the sweetest perfume on the planet. Everything about you turns me into a howling beast. You make me feel invincible, my love."

His praise not only vibrated over her flesh but also filled the deepest recesses of her heart.

"Would you like for me to bring your appetizers now, Sir?"

The waiter. Jesus Christ! Panic flooded her system as her eyes flew open wide. Ava tried to jerk away, but Quinn's embedded fingers held her in place. As the air in her lungs seized, she closed her eyes while her cheeks caught fire.

"Yes. That would be fine, thank you, Brice," Quinn replied without lifting from her thighs.

"Certainly, Mr. MacKinnon. However, I suspect the item you selected will pale in comparison to the delicacy you're enjoying now."

Ava swallowed back an irrational laugh as she listened to Brice retreat. Through half-lidded eyes, she gazed at the top of Quinn's head, savoring the sensations he granted.

Slowly, he raised his head and eased from inside her before locking eyes with her and licking her slippery nectar off his fingers. Pride twinkled in his moss-colored eyes. She felt treasured and adored, and a rush of peace flooded her soul. She'd never known the kind of love she and Quinn shared...the kind that encompassed every aspect of her being.

Her heart tripped when Quinn stood and placed his napkin on the edge of the table. A hungry look of longing flared in his eyes. Without a word, he gathered the entire bottom half of her dress, bunching it behind her back as he lifted her and set her butt on top of the table.

"Lay back for me, princess," he instructed before reaching down to lightly pet her pussy.

He wanted to have sex with her here? Here? Now? A flutter of excitement hummed inside her. She wanted to please Quinn in every way, but the indescribable thrill of being watched had slithered back into her veins.

"Hurry, pet. Unless you want me to wait until Brice returns before I devour your luscious pussy."

The slight smirk on his face told her Quinn intended to taunt her fantasy to the hilt. Her pulse quickened. Suddenly Ava realized being watched wasn't at all what she wanted. Her lurid fantasy was simply that...a fantasy. Living it out...well, she wasn't sure she could follow through with that.

Ava darted a quick glance over the restaurant.

"This isn't for you, princess. It's for me," he reminded, watching her keenly with a perceptive gaze.

Quinn had gone to great lengths to orchestrate this scene. Ava knew he wanted to seal the commitment and pledge of their Master/slave relationship. No way was she going to disappoint him. With a smile, she stared at his erotic features and blocked out the rest of the world. Ava centered her mind on Quinn and making all his kinky fantasies come true.

Ava eased her back onto the table, careful not to knock over the champagne glasses or disturb the gold-rimmed china place settings. The tips of her toes rested on the rich, earth-toned carpet as she watched Quinn's chest expand. His eyes sparkled with stark approval as he gazed down at her.

"So fucking beautiful," he murmured as he shoved the hem of her gown up over her chest that now heaved in anticipation.

Cool air wafted over her heated pussy, and her tunnel involuntarily clutched. Quinn tapped his fingers on her bare mound.

"Lift up for me, beautiful."

As she arched her hips, he tucked his napkin beneath her. Ava lay splayed out, totally exposed from the waist down. Her body rippled as a shiver raced up her spine. But the look of pride and love etched over Quinn's features pushed all her reservations aside.

"You make me so proud, princess," he cooed. "I love you, Ava."

"I love you, too, Master," she whispered with a brave smile.

She watched as Quinn lifted his glass of champagne. Expecting him to take a sip, she was startled when he tipped the flute and spilled the icy-cold bubbly over her sweltering folds. She yelped and jolted, but when he dipped his head between her legs and started lapping the chilly liquid from her pussy, Ava closed her eyes and moaned.

Lost in the sensation of his masterful tongue, flattened and laving the champagne-mixed-juices from her core, she marveled at his strong hands that gripped her thighs. Quinn held her open for his pleasure...and hers, and Ava didn't care if the waiter returned. Hell, she didn't care if the Dallas Cowboys football team sauntered in and circled the table to watch. All that mattered was pleasing Quinn.

Again, a trail of frigid liquid trickled down her sex, followed by the searing heat of his wicked tongue. As he licked and slurped the bubbly trail, her flesh warmed quickly from the heat of his mouth. Helpless, Ava rocked and writhed, whimpering pathetically as he ate at her like a madman. He thrust his tongue inside her fluttering tunnel while his thumb circled her pulsating clit. She issued a cry, then gripped her fists in his hair. Ava's eyes rolled back in her head. All she could do was hold on while Quinn tongue-fucked her to oblivion.

As he drove her to the edge, hard and fast, she arched her hips. Her breathless pleas echoed all around her. Quinn greedily imbibed her cunt and her control as he flung her headlong toward the peak of release. And as the familiar tingles of orgasm prickled outward, engulfing her limbs, Ava screamed out a plea for help.

But instead of granting her permission, Quinn stopped and raised his head.

Her eyes flew open wide as she watched him stand. A look of command lined his face as he licked her slick cream from his glistening lips. His eyes were glazed in need, and beneath the zipper of his dashing, formfitting tux, Ava spied his massive erection all but bursting to be free.

"No…oh, god. No. Please, Master. Please. You can't leave me like this," she whimpered.

Quinn arched a brow as he pinned her with a dubious stare. "Oh, but I can, my love. And I just did."

A string of obscenities lay on her tongue. Ava clenched her jaw to keep them from rolling past her lips as Quinn tugged the sodden napkin from beneath her. After folding the front of her dress back over her wet and throbbing sex, he extended his hand and helped her off the table.

Ava's entire body trembled as unmet demand careened

through her veins. When she went to stand, her knees nearly buckled out from under her, but Quinn snaked a strong arm around her waist before helping her back to her chair. He sat down across from her once again, and Ava dropped her gaze to the white linen tablecloth. Tears of frustration stung the backs of her eyes as she sucked in short, quivering breaths. How could he be so heartless…so mean…so damn tormenting? Where had his warm, loving, compassionate side gone?

"Look at me, princess."

Ava balked. She knew the minute her eyes locked with Quinn's he'd see the ugly emotions swirling inside her. It was at that instant that the waiter chose to return. She was thankful that he'd not reappeared a few seconds earlier, but also for the reprieve of Quinn's scrutiny. She needed a few quiet moments to wrangle her unsubmissive attitude.

Seemingly oblivious to either her or Quinn, the waiter kept his head tucked down while arranging a platter of plump, pink shrimp in the center of the table.

"Ava. Look at me," Quinn demanded in a sharp, stringent tone. "Or I'll invite Brice to stay and observe all that I have planned to do to you next instead of stealing glances of you from the kitchen."

She jerked her head upright. Darting a startled glance between the two men, Ava watched a slight, guilty smile tug the corners of the waiter's lips. Quinn studied her reaction with a laser-sharp eye before leaning back in his seat and crossing his steely arms over his wide chest. Damn him. Even his movements held a masculine kind of gracefulness she found arousing. Still, it did little to soothe the dejection and anxiety humming inside her, nor erase the embarrassment warming her cheeks knowing that she'd been watched.

CHAPTER SIX

QUINN WAS MIFFED that she chose to remain silent still, but the pink hue rising on her cheeks and the flicker of lust dancing in her eyes told Quinn that Ava was both mortified and turned on. While he had no idea if Brice had spied or not, Quinn honestly didn't care. Ava's conflicted reaction divulged how deep her exhibitionist streak truly ran. He arched his brows and held Ava's gaze while Brice refilled their glasses with champagne, waiting for her response. But she said nothing, only blushed a deeper shade of crimson.

Quinn waited until the waiter turned and walked away before issuing a heavy sigh. "Your submission shouldn't embarrass you, love. The desire to please shouldn't be hidden away like a dirty little secret, but worn proudly for the whole word to see. Hopefully before dinner is through, I can somehow convince you of that."

Ava nodded, nervously eying Brice until he was out of sight. "I know, I'm just afraid of what—"

"Of what people think?"

Quinn knew what insecurities lurked in her psyche. Over the years, he'd managed to vanquish many of her fears—most of them unrelated to the lifestyle—but now he wanted to eradicate the ones that held her prisoner from basking in their power exchange. He had to be certain she was with him for the long haul before the rest of his plans could be carried out.

"I'm not afraid of what people will think of me, Master," she declared, lifting her chin. "I'm afraid to inadvertently embarrass you and fail you in public. We've gone to great lengths to keep our relationship under wraps. I'd hate to do or say something to reveal our secret."

"Have you let it slip yet, girl?" he asked, ready to erase the worries she offered. "Have I ever once had to reprimand you for your behavior or comments?" She softly shook her head. "No. Have you ever failed me? Absolutely not. Do I think you might someday? Maybe, but I seriously doubt it. Do you want to know why?"

A glimmer of hope sprang over her face. "Why, Master?"

"Because the first night I saw you at Club Genesis—which, by the way, we are going to start visiting again, weekly—I saw the deep level of submission glowing inside you. Even when that prick, Kerr, tried to coerce you into scening with him and Mika stepped in, you held yourself with poise and grace," Quinn praised as he forked a shrimp from the plate and bit it in half.

A wry chuckle slid from her lips. "I wasn't exactly poised or graceful when I stepped into your office that following week, thinking I was interviewing with a stranger. The minute I realized it was you, I turned nearly turned tail and ran out of your building."

Quinn threw back his head and laughed. "That was one of the biggest *oh my god* moments of my entire life. I nearly swallowed my damn tongue when you came through my door. But when I saw how flustered and nervous you became, I could only focus on taking control and calming your fears."

She flashed him a wide, sexy smile. "And you've never stopped, Master. I think I fell in love with you a little bit that very day," she confessed shyly.

"It took you that long?" he asked in feigned shock. "I fell in love with you the first time I saw you at Genesis, my pet."

"You did not," she laughed.

"I did, too," he protested with a laugh, loving the playful banter between them. "I knew the minute I felt the overwhelming urge to rearrange Kerr's face that you'd instantly climbed inside my heart."

A flattered smiled curled her lips, and her eyes sparkled with happiness and pride. All through the scrumptious meal, they laughed and talked the way they used to when their relationship was new. It was a welcome respite for Quinn. He'd set aside all the pressures from work that loomed over his head and simply relaxed. He realized not only how easy it was to love Ava, but also how much he missed spending quality time—like this—with her. Proving even more that he needed to take charge and include this type of freedom to decompress with her each and every day.

When Brice returned with the dessert tray, Quinn watched as Ava's eyes lit up when she spied a decadent mountain of chocolate-black cherry cake.

"I'll take a cup of coffee and a slice of the chocolate cake, please," Quinn ordered.

The waiter turned to Ava. "And for you, ma'am?"

Just as she opened her mouth, Quinn, shook his head, then glanced back at the young man. "She'll take her dessert under the table, and we wish to not be disturbed, if you please."

Ava sucked in a tiny gasp, but Brice didn't even

acknowledge her reaction. Instead, the young waiter held Quinn's gaze and issued a professional nod. But as he turned to leave, the poor lad couldn't help but smile before striding away.

Quinn could almost feel the wheels spinning in her mind as Ava sat nervously nibbling her bottom lip. Good. He wanted her thinking...but on something other than embarrassment or her own self-confidence. He wanted her to string the meaning he'd intended behind the gloves engulfing her hands and her confinement, soon, beneath the table. She was a smart woman... She'd figure it out. At least he hoped she would.

Quinn cleared his throat. Ava lifted her eyes, leveling him with a pensive stare. His veins filled with the warmth of command knowing he'd ripped all semblance of security out from under her. Yes. That's what it was going to take for her unequivocal trust in him.

"Leave your gloves on and climb beneath the table. Position yourself on your knees at my feet, then release my zipper. You will take my fat cock into your sweet, hot mouth and worship it with every submissive cell in your body until you suck me dry."

Her moist, pink tongue slowly slid over her bottom lip. Quinn nearly embarrassed himself before she'd even had the chance to crawl under the table. God help him, the sultry minx would test his resolve to the nth degree, but he'd denied himself the pleasure of her velvety mouth long enough.

Ava stood, her body stiff and filled with apprehension. Quinn flashed her a lurid grin.

"Enjoy your dessert, my love. If you please me...as I have

all the faith that you will, I'll save you some cake."

She gave him a jerky nod before sweeping a long, nervous glance around the room. Ava sucked in a deep breath. Pride and lust pumped through his veins as he watched his brave and beautiful sub disappear beneath the table.

IF QUINN HAD told her, while she was getting dressed, that by the end of their meal Ava would be on and her hands and knees beneath the table of a five-star restaurant to give him a blow job, she would have laughed in his face. But now, on her knees with her eyes quickly adjusting to the light filtering in from under the tablecloth, staring at the slab of cock packed within his trousers, Ava didn't find an ounce of humor in her predicament. Nothing but a calm sense of serenity and purpose filled her.

Quinn spread his legs as she rested her butt on her heels. "You may begin," he instructed.

She hated the fact that she couldn't gaze up to see the hunger etched in his face...watch his eyes darken as she slid her tongue over his bulbous crest. He rocked his hips. Yes, Quinn was obviously running out of patience. And why wouldn't he be? He'd granted her permission to orgasm earlier. Quinn had been suffering now for hours and must be nearly bursting at the balls to come. Ava wanted nothing more than to put him out of his misery.

As she placed her gloved hands on the tops of his knees, his body heat leached through the fabric. She found the barrier between them cold and callous, making her feel almost alienated from him. She didn't like it. Ignoring her longing to actually feel his calming heat against her fingers, Ava leaned in and gently pressed her lips to the insides of his thighs. She slowly began working her way up both sides of his legs as she savored his heat against her lips.

"Your kisses are sweet, my pet. However, I don't remember instructing you to dawdle, did I?" Quinn asked in a low, sexy drawl.

"No, Sir," Ava replied with a smirk, weighing the thought of planting one more kiss before she got down to business. She loved tormenting him whenever she had the chance. Unfortunately with Quinn's Dominant mien, she rarely got that chance.

Reaching up, she released his leather belt and the top button of his trousers before carefully easing the zipper down. Holding her breath, Ava cupped his shaft in her gloved palm and eased his swollen erection past the metal teeth as his blood-engorged cock burst free. With a soft sigh of appreciation, she sat back on her heels and took several long seconds to simply gaze at his mouth-watering member.

It was hard, thick, and ribbed with copious veins, and his need reflected in the glistening bead poised at the tip of his wide crown. His pungent masculine musk hung so heavy within her shrouded cave Ava could almost taste him on her tongue.

Wrapping a gloved fist around his ready erection, she bit back a growl. The inability to feel his flesh irked her. With an inward groan of disappointment, she lifted her other hand and cupped his heavy sac, easing his balls from their confines as well. Heat rolled from between his parted legs like the summer sun, but it wasn't enough. Ava ached to feel his hot flesh in her hands.

"Your coffee and a nice thick slice of our trademark Chocolate Sin cake, sir."

Ava froze when the muffled voice of the waiter seeped under the table. Suddenly Quinn's words came thundering through her brain: *The desire to please shouldn't be hidden away like a dirty little secret but worn proudly for the whole word to see.* A wicked notion popped into her head, and Ava forced down the evil giggle bubbling up inside her. She planned to show him exactly how proud she was to be his submissive.

Opening her mouth wide, she plunged over his wide cock, taking his massive length all the way to the back of her throat in one big gulp. Quinn jolted, and a noise that sounded like a cough mixed with a moan rumbled from deep inside his chest, seemingly strangling in his throat. Ava released his cock with a soft snicker.

"Thank you," Quinn stated to the waiter, recovering quickly from her surprise attack.

"I'd extend an offer for you to enjoy your dessert, but I have a feeling you already are," Brice quipped with a chuckle.

"Like you can't fucking imagine," Quinn replied wholeheartedly.

Pride suffused Ava all the way to her toes as she opened once more and engulfed his glistening shaft. Quinn reached beneath the table and cupped the back of her neck, pressing her lips to the base of his cock. The cropped pubic hair tickled her nose, and long seconds passed as the breath trapped in her lungs began to burn. Silently alerting him to the fact she was running out of air, she gently rolled his balls in her palm, wishing she could feel his thin, soft skin ripple as it grew taut.

As Brice's footsteps retreated, Quinn loosened the grip at her nape. Ava slid back and inhaled a great gulp of air before sliding the tip of her tongue up and down his rippled veins. She could feel his thundering heartbeat pulsating on her tongue. Her pussy clutched as if jealous over his attention directed to her mouth. Licking him from stem to tip, Ava marveled not only at his addictive taste but at the power contained beneath the skin of his steely cock.

Flattening her tongue, she curled it around his bulbous crest, pausing to nibble and suck the sensitive spot beneath the heart-shaped flange. His clear, free-flowing emulsion dripped past her lips and onto her tongue. Lost in the velvety slick textures, Ava issued a contented sigh.

"Be aware, the more you toy with me, girl, the longer I'll make you suffer once I get you back to our room. Trust me. You won't like it, either," Quinn warned with a growl.

Several seconds later, a tempting moan vibrated through his body and reverberated over her busy lips.

"This cake is sinful, pet. Of course nothing can compare to your sweet mouth. However, if you don't stop taunting me and suck the come from my aching balls, I won't leave you a damn morsel."

Ava couldn't care less about cake at that moment. She was too enthralled with pumping her mouth up and down and swirling her tongue over every inch of him. All she wanted to do was feel his hot seed erupt down her throat.

Her pussy wept and her body tingled. Flames of desire licked up her spine and singed her veins while the stupid gloves distracted her more with each passing second. She hated how they stole her connection to Quinn. Yes, the sensation of him on her tongue was euphoric. Still, worshiping his cock this way felt muted and dulled, taking from her enjoyment. Why did he insist she wear the damn things anyway? They were stifling and confining like the veil of linen encasing her in this private tomb.

Ava longed to strip the irritating fabric away, toss the glove aside, and lay her bare hands on him…drink in all his familiar and exotic textures. She wanted to throw back the tablecloth, as well. The fact that she couldn't watch the pleasure flutter over his face only increased the growing chasm disconnecting her from him. Though disenchanted, she didn't stop servicing his cock with gusto even while the act felt sterile and void of their loving and sensual bond.

Quinn had spent a great deal of time and money planning their special time together, but why? What did he seek from her? What did he expect to gain from this impersonal, near public display of her submission? As a litany of questions careened through her brain, she dutifully sucked and swirled, determined to bring him all the pleasure she could give.

"Deeper, princess. Take me down that silky throat of yours." Ava complied as Quinn groaned. "Swallow around me…oh, yes. That's it."

His gravelly tone left no doubt in her mind that she was indeed pleasing him, but without seeing the visible rapture on his face, shards of isolation pierced her heart.

The linen cloth separating them felt like a solid wall of marble. If Quinn wanted her to wear her submission proudly, for the whole world to see, why had he hidden her beneath the table? His words and actions clashed, like enemies on a battlefield. How could she openly bask in her submission while keeping their professional reputations free from jeopardy? It couldn't be done.

So why had Quinn so brazenly splayed her out on the table and devoured her for the whole world to see? Technically there'd only been a skeleton crew to service their meal; still, his actions made no sense. Ava could still feel the cold champagne and Quinn's warm tongue lapping at her cunt. A shiver of delight tore through her musings, but only for a few short seconds. Her brain engaged once more, trying to analyze the strange Dominance Quinn had displayed over the past several hours. As she split her focus between the task at hand—or rather mouth—and the need to bend to an unfamiliar submission, the puzzle pieces slowly started coming together.

Quinn had purposefully remained silent when he joined her in their hotel room. He'd wanted her to think she was giving a lewd masturbation show to some unknown stranger. Why else would he have remained quiet? But why? Was it all some kind of test to see if she'd freak the hell out? Which she had. Even after failing him, Ava had willingly accepted his punishment—the harshest Quinn had ever doled out. She thought she'd paid her penance. So why did she feel as if he'd extended her sentence?

"You're not focusing, princess. Do I need to drag you onto the table once more?"

Quinn's low grumble drew her from her thoughts. Ava directed her attention to his cock, working her mouth up and down with renewed vigor. She was rewarded with his guttural moans of pleasure and soft-spoken praises. Still, her mind continued to search for the meaning behind his peculiar Dominance. Her thoughts spooled once more to him blatantly putting her on display. It wasn't like him to openly fondle her in a public setting, let alone drink champagne from her pussy on top of the table.

Suddenly, a light bulb illuminated her brain.

Quinn wanted to cast off the cloak of secrecy and expose their relationship.

The blindfold, the gloves, the table linen that concealed her…they were all symbols of their relationship. Exposing her to an imaginary stranger, then doing so again, for real, here in the restaurant, Quinn was asking her if she was ready to reveal not only her submission but their love and commitment to the whole world.

Yes. Yes. A thousand times, yes.

Ava's heart soared. Throwing caution to the wind, she stripped off her gloves. Tossing back the edge of the tablecloth, Ava boldly raised her eyes. Meeting Quinn's startled gaze, she placed her bare hands on his naked flesh, and her whole world righted itself once more.

A slow, lazy smile spread over his luscious lips as Quinn reached down and caressed the hollow of her cheek with his knuckles. Unadulterated pride etched his face, and Ava felt as if she were melting like a snow cone in August.

Nuzzling into his touch, she savored the heat that engulfed her palms and enveloped her fingers. Staring up at his heavy lids, she drank in the smoldering reflection of love, lust, and need as she cradled his tightly drawn sac. Worshiping his steely cock, Ava strived to convey to him all the love she felt exploding inside her.

The connection she'd desperately longed for beneath the table blossomed like a living electrical current. The energy pulsed between them, igniting every cell in her body and filling her with a renewed warmth and deeper kind of love.

"My beautiful Ava, you've figured out my motives, haven't

you?"

"Mmm," she moaned around his shaft while nodding her head.

"Are you ready for the world to know you're mine, princess?"

Ava nodded once more while pride and passion swamped her.

"We'll now have the freedom to be who and what we are from here on out. Is that what you want, as well?"

Ava released him just long enough to whisper a desperate "yes" before drawing his glistening, hot shaft into her mouth once again.

"Thank god," Quinn exhaled loudly.

Without warning, he gripped his hands into her hair. Ava's scalp tingled, and her body quivered as Quinn took control. Rapidly pumping past her lips, he drove demandingly all the way to the back of her throat. She felt his shaft swell even larger over her tongue before he jerked free. With a sense of urgency, Quinn shoved away from the table and stood. Ava's lips and mouth mourned the loss of his hardness, but his familiar taste remained branded on her tongue. With a feral growl, he bent and lifted her from the floor before plopping her onto the table. All the while, she kept her eyes locked with his as he hastily reached beneath her dress. Running his wide, warm hands up her legs, he skimmed his palms up her thighs, dragging her dress along with them. Quinn didn't stop until he'd uncovered her wet and ready pussy. Only then did he break their gaze to settle a stare on her sex.

With a feral growl, he clutched her thighs and spread her legs wide before gripping a hand on her hip. Fisting his other around his cock, Quinn aligned the dripping tip to her folds.

Like a man possessed, he drove into her slick, quivering tunnel as a roar rumbled from his chest.

"Mine," he bellowed as he began maniacally pumping into her. "My sweet princess... My brave slave... My beautiful, glorious, Ava. Mine...all mine."

His eyes blazed in a fire of possessiveness she'd never seen before. Quinn resembled an animal, wild and untamed. But Ava wasn't afraid. No, she was too consumed by the fire rising inside to do anything but cast her inhibitions aside and rut with the beast who owned her heart...her soul.

Pride burst inside her as the air in her lungs constricted. "Yes. Yours. All yours," she breathlessly cried.

Quinn's eyes narrowed as he slid his palm to the back of her neck and slanted his mouth over hers in a raw, spine-bending kiss. Ava whimpered and wrapped her legs around his narrow waist, locking her ankles at the small of his back while their tongues dueled in passion and desire.

He ate at her mouth with the same fury that matched his thrusts...as if he wanted to climb inside her soul and stay there for all time. And that's exactly where she wanted to be, as well.

Ava writhed against his pubic bone as it ground against her clit. The wide crest of his cock stroked the sensitive bundle of nerves buried inside her, fueling her need to a desperate level. Soaring higher and higher, Ava prayed she'd never come back down.

Heat poured off his body, surrounding her in a blanket of warmth and safety. Everything around her fell away except for Quinn and the mounting need to please him. Peeling off the layers that had encased their love felt liberating. All Ava wanted to do was meld herself to him...mesh her body, heart, and soul to Quinn's for now and forever.

CHAPTER SEVEN

QUINN'S HEAD SPUN at the feel of her arching and meeting his thrusts, and the sound of her soft gasps spilling from her lips. He wanted to slow down and make love to her tenderly, but the beast inside seemed to possess him with a single-mindedness. He couldn't let up...couldn't hold back the rush of joy and pent up demand surging through him.

The friction of her tight cunt burned his cock, and the seed churning in his balls singed his flesh from the inside out. Quinn struggled to contain the blistering fire, but once Ava began whimpering in her familiar kitten-like moans, he was gone.

"Now, princess. Come for me. Come hard. Now," he roared as his cock expanded and his vision blurred.

Desire and demand coalesced in a blinding explosion, his eruption so powerful Quinn felt the vibration blast up his spine, buckling his knees as they shattered in unison. Spasms sent his seed jettisoning and surging as Ava's velvety tunnel clutched and milked around him in a sublime and brutal grip. Blinking through the haze that enveloped his brain, Quinn stared at Ava as she splintered beneath him and screamed out his name. A sight so thrilling and heady he vowed to spend the rest of his life coaxing her to one glorious crescendo after another.

As her quivering cunt continued to suck him dry, Quinn wrapped his arm around her waist and pulled her to his chest. Their hearts pounded in a thundering rhythm, as aftershocks rippled and jolted through their bodies. Ava's panting breaths licked at his neck as she wrapped her arms around him. Quinn closed his eyes, savoring the sweet bliss of her in his arms as they slowly floated back to earth.

After several long moments, their breathing leveled out, and Quinn gently eased from inside her. Tucking his cock away, he drew a handkerchief from his back pocket and gently wiped her wet, swollen folds. Ava stared up at him beneath heavy eyelids wearing a dazed and sated expression. And when she sent him a shy, sweet smile, he leaned over and pressed a soft kiss on her ripe lips. Pulling back slightly, he dragged his cinnamon-colored whiskers down her neck. Ava giggled and hunched her shoulders to ward off his tickling scruff.

"Can we go back to the room and do that again?" she asked on a dreamy sigh.

"Not yet, princess. There's still one surprise I have in store. That is, if you have the strength to stand and walk with me," he teased.

"You're good, MacKinnon...err, I mean Master," she corrected with a tiny giggle. "But as you can plainly see, I *am* still conscious."

"Then let's go, so we can get back and I can make love to you until you're no longer conscious."

Ava purred in delight as he extended his hand and helped her from the table. With his arm around her waist, he escorted her toward the door.

"Wait. We didn't pay for dinner," Ava stated with a worried look.

"It was paid in full before we ever arrived."

She gave him a sideways glance and narrowed her eyes. "So Brice wasn't going to come back to our table after he delivered dessert, was he?"

"Nope." Quinn grinned. Pulling her to a stop, he delved deep into her eyes. "Did you want him to?"

"No." Ava shook her head. "You're the only man I want watching me…touching me…loving me. I love you."

"I love you, too, my beautiful Ava."

Quinn splayed his hand over the small of her back as he led her to the elevator. A blast of anxiety washed through his veins as he pressed the button that would take them to the final surprise he had in store. Brushing aside his unease, he pulled Ava snuggly against his side while he slipped his other hand into the pocket of his tux.

When the doors opened, Quinn led Ava to a small fountain in the center of the room before helping her take a seat on the white marble ledge. As he cupped her chin, she stared up at him, happiness sparkling in her hazel eyes. Unable to resist the tempting bow of her lips, he bent and brushed his mouth over hers while plucking out the blue velvet box from his pocket.

Pulling back, he stared at the contours of her face, drinking in her exquisite beauty. Gliding his thumb over her bottom lip, he swallowed the lump suddenly lodged in his throat. "I love you, Ava. You not only make me the proudest Master on the planet but the happiest man, as well. Still, I'm not yet fully satisfied."

He watched as the glowing smile vanished from her face. A look of panic flashed in her eyes, and Ava suddenly grew tense.

"What more can I give you, Sir?" she asked in a soft, worried voice.

Quinn paused and sent her a reassuring smile wishing he felt as confident as he appeared. For the first time in his life, doubt and fear had him in a stranglehold. If Ava wasn't ready, he wasn't quite sure what he would do. How he'd react. Of course, he'd had plenty of conversations with himself over the past few months...wanting this, but not one hundred percent sure Ava did. Dammit. This wasn't the time to start second-guessing...not now. He'd come too far, brought her into the light where he wanted their relationship to be...well, almost.

Ava's bottom lip quivered, and Quinn silently cursed himself for his extended silence. With a shake of his head, he brushed his hand over her cheek and gave her a nervous smile. "There's only one thing more that would make my life complete." He lifted his palm, noticing that his hand was shaking, and opened the lid on the little blue box. As he dropped to one knee before her, Ava sucked in a startled breath as she stared dumbfounded at the shimmering diamond ring. Tears sprang from her eyes as she glanced up at him with a stunned expression.

It was now or never.

"I'll only kneel this once before you, my love...as this is your place...at my feet, by my side, and bound to my heart...forever. You complete me in ways I can't begin to put into words. But I will spend the rest of my life showing you, in every way possible, the depth of love I hold in my heart for you. I want you in my life, sweetheart...as my slave, my lover and friend, but most importantly, as my wife. Ava Gibbs, will you marry me?"

Tears streamed down her face. Quinn held his breath. It seemed an interminable amount of time before she began nodding, and even longer before a strangled "yes" bubbled from the back of her throat.

All the tension exploded from within. Blinking back his own tears, Quinn thought his heart was going to burst from his chest as he slid the three-carat diamond ring onto her trembling finger.

"Oh, Quinn," she sobbed. "It's so beautiful. I love you...love you more than you'll ever know."

Ava threw her arms around his neck and kissed him. Kissed him with a fiery passion that both calmed his fears and boiled his blood. She had the unique talent to do that to him, but then, it was only one of the many reasons he was so damn in love with her.

"Then let's do this." He winked with a laugh, nodding toward the tiny wedding chapel beyond the fountain.

"What? Here?" She blinked. "Now? Are you serious?"

His heart clutched and he sobered, staring down at her intently. "Unless you're having second thoughts or reservations... Are you?"

Please don't let her say yes. He sent up a silent prayer as he tensed and waited for her reply.

"Are you kidding? No. Not a one," she laughed. Sniffing, she blotted the tears from beneath her lashes.

With an inward fist pump, Quinn bit back a cheer. Cupping her face, he drank in the happiness sparkling in her eyes, lighting up her smile, and glowing on her cheeks. Pressing his lips to hers, he kissed her...kissed her with the promise to keep her on her submissive toes while guiding and protecting her, but most of all with a vow to love her unconditionally until the end of time.

"Oh, my… I can't believe this is happening," she giggled.

"Believe it, my love. I've been waiting for this moment longer than you can imagine."

She cocked her head and gaped at him. "How long have you waited?" she quizzed.

"Since the first time I saw you at Club Genesis," he confessed.

Ava's eyes grew wide and her mouth dropped open. "You're teasing, right?"

"Nope." He laughed, then wrapped his arm around her waist.

"Quinn MacKinnon, you are full of surprises," Ava mockingly scolded.

"Oh, princess…you have no idea the surprises I have in store for you tonight."

He wrapped his arm around her waist as his chest expanded with pride. Stepping onto the red carpet that led to the quaint chapel, Quinn couldn't wipe the smile from his lips.

"Okay, but if you plan to claim me in the lobby or anything like that, I'm going to have to call my safeword," she whispered as they stepped inside.

"No, princess. From now on, you're for my eyes only."

ABOUT THE AUTHOR

USA Today Bestselling author **Jenna Jacob** paints a canvas of passion, romance, and humor as her alpha men and the feisty women who love them unravel their souls, heal their scars, and find a happy-ever-after kind of love. Heart-tugging, captivating, and steamy, Jenna's books will surely leave you breathless and craving more.

A mom of four grown children, Jenna and her alpha-hunk husband live in Kansas. She loves reading, getting away from the city on the back of a Harley, music, camping, and cooking.

Meet her wild and wicked fictional family in Jenna's sultry series: ***The Doms of Genesis.*** Become spellbound by searing triple love connections in her continuing saga: ***The Doms of Her Life*** (co-written with the amazing Shayla Black and Isabella La Pearl). Journey with couples struggling to resolve their pasts and heal their scars to discover unbridled love and devotion in her contemporary series: ***Passionate Hearts***. Or laugh along as Jenna lets her zany sense of humor and lack of filter run free in the romantic comedy series: ***Hotties of Haven***.

Connect with Jenna Online
Website: www.jennajacob.com
Email: jenna@jennajacob.com
Facebook Fan Page: facebook.com/authorjennajacob
Twitter: @jennajacob3
Instagram: instagram.com/jenna_jacob_author
Amazon Author Page: http://amzn.to/1GvwNnn
Newsletter: http://bit.ly/1Cj4ZyY

OTHER TITLES BY JENNA JACOB

The Doms of Genesis Series
Embracing My Submission
Masters of My Desire
Master of My Mind
Saving My Submission
Seduced By My Doms
Lured By My Master
Sin City Submission
Bound To Surrender
Resisting My Submission (March 21, 2017)
Craving His Command (May 23, 2017)

The Doms of Her Life – Raine Falling Series
(Co-authored with Shayla Black and Isabella LaPearl)
One Dom To Love
The Young and The Submissive
The Bold and The Dominant
The Edge Of Dominance

The Passionate Hearts Series
Sky Of Dreams
Winds Of Desire (Coming Soon)

Hotties Of Haven Series
Sin On A Stick
Wet Dream